Scientific Method Investigation

A Step-by-Step Guide for Middle-School Students

BY
SCHYRLET CAMERON, CAROLYN CRAIG,
and SHERRYL SOUTEE

COPYRIGHT © 2009 Mark Twain Media, Inc.

ISBN 978-1-58037-521-4

Printing No. CD-404118

Mark Twain Media, Inc., Publishers
Distributed by Carson-Dellosa Publishing LLC

Visit us at www.carsondellosa.com

Table of Contents

Introduction to the Teacher

Scientific Method Investigation is designed to promote scientific literacy. The National Science Education Standards recommend teaching inquiry using the steps in the scientific method. Learning this process is vital in enabling students to become problem solvers in everyday life. Unfortunately, most textbooks only devote one chapter to explaining and demonstrating these steps. In other chapters, science activities or experiments are often used to clarify or reinforce concepts presented in the text, but they leave out the important steps in the scientific method.

Scientific Method Investigation provides teachers with a wide range of lessons that follow the scientific method from start to finish. Chapters are organized to engage students in authentic science learning associated with physical, life, earth, and space science. The experimental investigations encourage students to develop an understanding of the concepts and processes of science through the use of good scientific techniques. Each section can be used as a "stand-alone" unit or to supplement and enrich the content area. The book provides students with:

- step-by-step procedures for scientific problem solving. Traditional labs provide guided inquiry as students hypothesize, plan investigations, collect and analyze data, and formulate conclusions.

- a basic review of the metric system for data collection. Students have many opportunities to practice their mathematical skills as they collect data for the experimental investigations provided in each chapter.

- clear directions for using scientific equipment. Investigations offer students opportunities to practice data-collection skills using lab equipment such as the triple-beam balance, graduated cylinder, spring scale, and thermometers.

- easy-to-understand format for identifying the variables when setting up a controlled experimental investigation.

- tips for creating, exhibiting, and presenting a science fair project. The inquiry lab format challenges students to design their own experiments using the steps in the scientific method.

Scientific Method Investigation supports the No Child Left Behind (NCLB) Act. The book promotes student knowledge and understanding of science and mathematics concepts through inquiry learning. The activities are designed to strengthen scientific literacy skills that are correlated to the National Science Education Standards (NSES) and the National Council for Mathematics Standards (NCTM).

How to Use the Book

Scientific Method Investigation is designed to make it easy for the teacher to plan and facilitate laboratory activities in the science classroom. It is intended to help foster student confidence regarding scientific investigations through skill building. The book also provides students with basic information and practice using the scientific method, laboratory equipment, and measurement techniques before actually beginning experimental investigations in the classroom.

Strategies
Chapter 1—Foster student confidence regarding scientific investigations
Student Skill Building
- Introduce the scientific method and focus on the importance of each step. Learning this process helps students become better problem solvers.
- Demonstrate correct handling procedures for equipment. Following proper techniques when using laboratory equipment helps prevent accidents.
- Review the SI units and metric system. Student success in data collection is increased as they improve their measurement skills.

Chapters 2, 3, and 4—Practice the process of scientific problem solving
Teacher Preparation
- Read through the investigation carefully.
- Analyze the investigation for appropriateness for your students.
- Determine approximately how long the investigation will take.
- Perform the activity yourself so that you can determine where students may have trouble.

Classroom Investigation
- Read through the investigation with students.
- Instruct students to follow directions carefully.
- Require students to wear appropriate clothing and protective equipment.
- Review safety practices.
- Demonstrate the proper use of science equipment to be used.

Chapter 5—Design and conduct a scientific investigation
Middle School Science Fair
- Read through the planning, completion, and presentation steps with students.
- Review project ideas. Direct students to select a topic of interest to them.
- Monitor students' progress to guarantee all projects are completed by the required date.
- Encourage parental involvement.

National Standards

National Science Education Standards (NSES)
National Research Council (1996). National Science Education Standards. Washington, D.C.: National Academy Press.

Science as Inquiry
Content Standard A: As a result of activities in grades 5–8, all students should develop
- abilities necessary to do scientific inquiry.
- understandings about scientific inquiry.

Physical Science
Content Standard B: As a result of activities in grades 5–8, all students should develop an understanding of
- properties of objects and materials.
- motions and forces.
- transfer of energy.

Life Science
Content Standard C: As a result of activities in grades 5–8, all students should develop an understanding of
- structure and function in living systems.
- reproduction and heredity.
- populations and ecosystems.
- diversity and adaptations of organisms.

Earth and Space Science
Content Standard D: As a result of activities in grades 5–8, all students should develop an understanding of
- structure of the earth system.
- Earth's history.
- Earth in the solar system.

National Council for Teachers of Mathematics Standards (NCTM)
National Council for Teachers of Mathematics (2000). Principles and Standards for School Mathematics. Reston, VA: National Council for Teachers of Mathematics.

Measurement
- In grades 5–8, students should be able to understand measurable attributes of objects and the units, systems, and processes of measurement.
- In grades 5–8, students should be able to apply appropriate techniques, tools, and formulas to determine measurements.

Name: _____ Date: _____

Chapter 1   # The Scientific Method

Scientific inquiry is a process scientists use to find answers to questions they have about the world around them. They use the steps in the **scientific method** to design and conduct scientific investigations to explore possible answers.

Steps in the scientific method answer a question.
1. Purpose: What do you want to learn from the experiment?
2. Research: What is already known about the topic?
3. Hypothesis: What do you think will happen in the experiment?
4. Procedure: How will you test the hypothesis and record the results?
5. Analysis: What do the results tell about the experiment?
6. Conclusion: Do the results support your hypothesis?

Test Yourself

I. A **mnemonic device** is a special word or phrase used to help a person remember something, particularly lists. Create a mnemonic device for the steps in the scientific method.

Steps	Example	Your Mnemonic
Purpose	**P**eter	**P**
Research	**R**abbit	**R**
Hypothesis	**H**ates	**H**
Procedure	**P**eas	**P**
Analysis	**A**nd	**A**
Conclusion	**C**arrots	**C**

II. Write the question asked for each step in the scientific method.

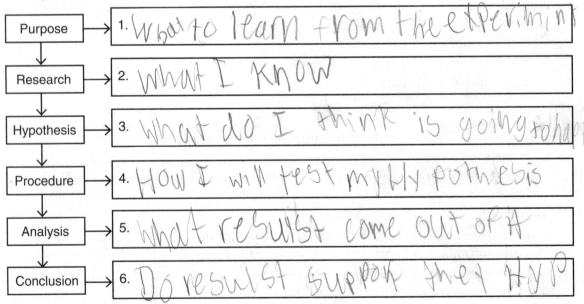

Purpose → 1. What to learn from the experiment

Research → 2. What I know

Hypothesis → 3. What do I think is going to happen

Procedure → 4. How I will test my hypothesis

Analysis → 5. What results come out of it

Conclusion → 6. Do results support they Hyp

Name: _____ Date: _____

The Scientific Method—Purpose   `Chapter 1`

Scientists are problem solvers. They ask many questions about what they see going on in their world. They conduct scientific investigations to find the answers to these questions. Most investigations follow a general pattern.

Choosing a Topic for Investigation

A good topic is one that can be tested with an experiment. It is important that the topic is not too general.

Example: <u>Too General</u>   <u>Good Topic</u>
meal worms   food meal worms eat

Stating the Purpose

Scientists explain exactly what they want to learn from their investigation in the purpose. The purpose is written as a question, often called the "Big Question." The purpose of an investigation includes three components. (1) It is clearly written. (2) It usually starts with the verb "does." (3) It can be answered by measuring something.

Example: <u>Topic</u>   <u>Purpose (What do you want to learn about the topic?)</u>
plant growth rates   Does fertilizer affect the growth rate of a plant?
fireflies' flash rates   Does temperature affect the flash rate of fireflies?
paper airplanes' design   Does the design of a paper airplane affect its hang time?

Test Yourself

I.   Decide which topics are good ideas and which are too general for scientific investigation. Record your answers below.

Topic	Too General /Good
1. best brand of batteries	GOOD
2. volcanoes around the world	TOO
3. water conservation	TOO
4. materials used as insulators	GOOD

II.   Practice writing a purpose for each topic. Record your answers below. Remember to start the purpose with the word "Does."

Topic	Purpose
1. temperature and bread mold	dose bread mold diffrctly with temp
2. texture of paper towels	do paper towels fell diffrnt
3. colored light and plant growth	dose colerd ligh efect plun groth
4. light and the activity of meal worms	dose ligh efect meal worms
5. rust and the strength of magnets	dose a magnet stick to rust

Name: _____ Date: _____

Chapter 1   The Scientific Method—Research

Before carrying out any experiment, a scientist finds out what is already known about the topic being investigated. A good starting point is to identify the key words in the purpose. Next, look up each key word in an encyclopedia, dictionary, or textbook. Then, expand the research to the Internet.

Example: Does fertilizer affect the growth rate of a sunflower?

The goal of the search is to find information that will help in forming a prediction about what will occur in the experiment. Scientists use questions to direct their investigations.

Fertilizer

Why do we need fertilizers?
How do fertilizers affect plant growth?
Who invented fertilizer?
What are the ingredients in fertilizers that affect plant growth?
When do plants need fertilizer?
Where should fertilizer be applied to the plant to get the best results?

Sunflowers

Why does soil type affect plant growth?
How do minerals and nutrients affect plant growth?
Who would be a good resource in my community to contact about plants?
What are the elements required for plant growth?
When does photosynthesis affect plant growth?
Where in the plant does photosynthesis occur?

Test Yourself

I.   Underline the key words for each purpose below.
   1.   Does the depth a seed is planted affect its ability to sprout?
   2.   Does eating breakfast affect short-term memory?

II. Write questions to direct the research for the purpose: Does temperature affect the strength of a magnet?

Temperature	Magnet
1. Why	1. Why
2. How	2. How
3. Who	3. Who
4. What	4. What
5. When	5. When
6. Where	6. Where

Name: _____ Date: _____

The Scientific Method—Hypothesis   Chapter 1

After completing the research, a scientist is able to make an educated guess or prediction about what will happen in the experiment. This prediction is called the **hypothesis**. A clearly written hypothesis follows a set pattern. It answers the question stated in the purpose. It is brief and to the point. It uses the same word pattern as the purpose.

Example: Purpose: Does the <u>depth</u> of a <u>seed</u> affect its <u>sprouting time</u>?
Hypothesis: An increase of the <u>depth</u> of a <u>seed</u> will increase its <u>sprouting time</u>.

The hypothesis is worded so that it can be tested. It identifies the independent variable and dependent variable. These variables are often referred to as factors, traits, or conditions. The terms increase and decrease are often used to predict what will happen in the experiment.

- **Independent Variable:** The factor that is changed in an experiment. (depth of seed)
- **Dependent Variable:** The factor that responds to the change. The change is measured and recorded in metric units. (sprouting time)

Example: Hypothesis: Warmer **water temperatures** will increase the **amount of sugar** dissolved.
Independent Variable: water temperature
Dependent Variable: amount of sugar that dissolves, measured in grams

Test Yourself

I.   Write a hypothesis for each purpose.
   1. Purpose: Does fertilizer affect the growth rate of a plant?
      Hypothesis: _____

   2. Purpose: Does air pressure affect the height a basketball will bounce?
      Hypothesis: _____

   3. Purpose: Does age affect the heart rate of humans?
      Hypothesis: _____

II. Identify the independent and dependent variables for each hypothesis below.
   1. Hypothesis: Warmer water temperatures will increase the heart rate of fish.
      Independent Variable: _____
      Dependent Variable: _____

   2. Hypothesis: The design of a paper airplane will affect the distance traveled.
      Independent Variable: _____
      Dependent Variable: _____

   3. Hypothesis: More light will increase the movement of meal worms.
      Independent Variable: _____
      Dependent Variable: _____

Name: _____ Date: _____

 **The Scientific Method—Procedure**

The **procedure** is a step-by-step set of directions for testing the hypothesis. A good procedure is so detailed and complete that other scientists can duplicate the experiment. The procedure includes several components.

Materials: Materials are a list of items needed to conduct the experiment. The list is written similar to a recipe. Materials and supplies are listed in the order they are to be used in the experiment. Measurements are written using metric units.

Experiment: The experiment is a test designed to answer the question stated in the purpose. The test consists of two groups.

- Experimental Group: This group includes the part or parts of the experiment that are changed and tested. The results are then compared to the control group to determine what changes have taken place.
- Control Group: This group includes the part or parts of the experiment that are left unchanged. The conditions a scientist wants to remain the same during the experiment are called **constants**.

Variables: When conducting a test, scientists change certain things and then observe how they affect the experiment. These "things" are called variables. The variables in an experiment are often referred to as factors, traits, or conditions. An experiment usually has two variables.

- Independent Variable: The factor that is changed and tested in the experiment. A good experiment has only one independent variable.
- Dependent Variable: The factor that responds to the change. The change is measured and recorded in metric units.

Data: Data is a record of the results of the experiment, and it is usually recorded in a data table. Later, the data is organized in a graph to make the information easy to read and analyze.

Test Yourself

I.   Matching

    _____ 1.   data   a. the items needed to conduct an experiment

    _____ 2.   variable   b. a test designed to answer the question in the purpose

    _____ 3.   experiment c. a record of the results observed in an experiment

    _____ 4.   materials   d. a factor that can be changed and tested in an experiment

II. Fill in the Blanks

1. The _____ is a step-by-step set of directions for testing the hypothesis.

2. A good experiment has only _____ independent variable.

3. Changes in the _____ _____ are measured with the metric system.

4. The _____ is organized in a graph to make it easy to read and analyze.

5. During the experiment, the data is usually recorded in a _____ _____.

Name: _____ Date: _____

The Scientific Method—Data   Chapter 1

A scientist keeps a careful record of the data collected during an experiment. The results are often organized in a data table. A table is divided into columns and rows. It includes a title, clearly labeled parts, units of measurement are identified, and if appropriate, the average (mean) for different trials is included.

Hypothesis: Warmer water temperatures will increase the respiration rate of fish.

Respiration Rate of Guppies
(Breaths per minute)

Temperature of Water	Trial #1 Respiration Rate	Trial #2 Respiration Rate	Trial #3 Respiration Rate	Trial #4 Respiration Rate	Average (Mean)
20°C	78	78	77	79	78
24°C	120	124	122	126	123
26°C	170	180	161	177	172
28°C	201	202	203	202	202

*Respiration rate was determined by counting the number of times the fish's gills opened in one minute.

Finding the Average

The mean is the average of a set of numbers. To calculate the average, add up all the numbers in the set, and then divide by how many numbers there are in the set. (Remember: It is the *sum* divided by the *count*.)

Example: What is the average of these numbers? 78, 78, 77, 79
- Step #1: Add the numbers: 78 + 78 + 77 + 79 = 312 (sum)
- Step #2: Divide the sum by how many numbers were added (4 numbers were added): 312 ÷ 4 = 78
- Step # 3: Identify the average: The average is 78.

Test Yourself
Complete the data table by finding the average.

Height of Ball Bounce

Air Pressure	Trial #1	Trial #2	Trial #3	Trial #4	Average (Mean)
4 PSI (lbs.)	53 cm	53 cm	52 cm	54 cm	1.
6 PSI (lbs.)	66 cm	68 cm	70 cm	64 cm	2.
8 PSI (lbs.)	122 cm	126 cm	128 cm	124 cm	3.
12 PSI (lbs.)	176 cm	167 cm	175 cm	174 cm	4.

Chapter 1   # The Scientific Method—Analysis

After scientists complete an experiment, they need to decide what the results mean. They often organize their data using a graph. A graph makes it easy to read the results of the experiment and identify patterns. Most kinds of graphs have the same basic parts.

Basic Parts of a Graph

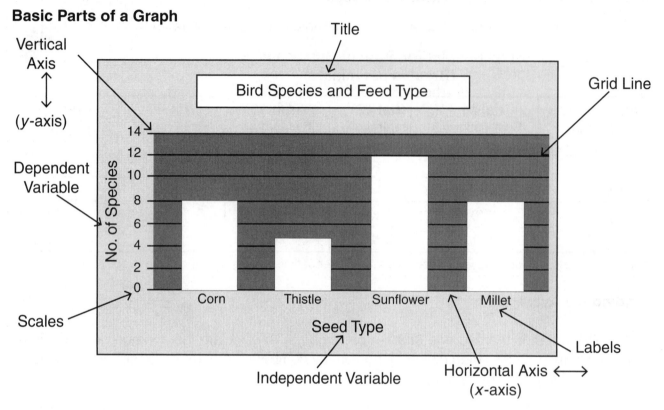

Graph Title: The graph title gives an overview of the information being presented in the graph. The title is given at the top of the graph.

Axes and Their Labels: Each graph has two axes. The labels indicate what information is presented on each axis.

- Horizontal axis (*x*-axis)–Independent Variable: the factor that is changed or tested by the experimenter
- Vertical axis (*y*-axis)–Dependent Variable: the factor that responds to the change

Scale: The range of values being represented is placed at **equal** intervals along the vertical axis. Numbers on the scale are lined up with the grid lines. Do not place numbers in between the lines.

Name: _____ Date: _____

The Scientific Method—Analysis (cont.)   Chapter 1

Three Types of Graphs

Graph #1

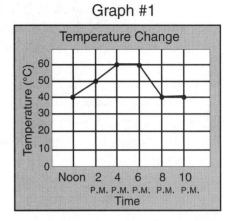

Different types of graphs are appropriate for different experiments. Three common types of graphs are line, bar, and circle.

Line Graph: A line graph is used to show how data changes over time. Both variables in a line graph must be numbers. One variable (time) is shown on the horizontal axis (←→), or x-axis, of the graph. The other variable (temperature) is placed along the vertical axis (↕), or y-axis. The data is connected by a rising or falling line. The line shows changes or trends usually over time.

Graph #2

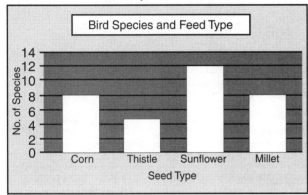

Bar Graph: A bar graph uses bars to show the relationship among the variables. It can be drawn either horizontally (←→) or vertically (↕). A bar graph is used to compare results that are totals, such as time, width, distance, temperature, height, and length. One variable is shown on the horizontal axis, or x-axis, of the graph. The other variable is placed along the vertical axis, or y-axis.

Graph #3
Earth's Atmosphere

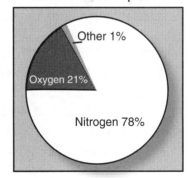

Circle Graph: A circle graph is used to show percentage or fractions of the whole. Circle graphs are sometimes called pie charts. Each slice of the pie represents a fraction of the total.

Test Yourself
Analyze the data represented in each graph above. What do the results tell you?

Graph #1: _____

_____

Graph #2: _____

_____

Graph #3: _____

_____

Name: _____ Date: _____

 **The Scientific Method—Conclusion**

A scientist carefully studies the data collected during a scientific investigation. The information is used to write a **conclusion** that summarizes the results of the experiment. It includes the purpose, a brief description of the procedure, and whether or not the hypothesis was supported by the data. Scientists use key facts from their research to help explain the results.

Sometimes scientists find that the results do not support their hypothesis. When this happens, they don't change or manipulate the results to fit their hypothesis. Scientists do not consider negative results as bad. They just explain why things did not go as expected. They use the negative results as the first step in constructing a new hypothesis and designing a new experiment.

Test Yourself

Study the hypothesis and results of the scientific investigations below. Write a conclusion that summarizes the results of the experiment. Does the information support the hypothesis?

I.   Hypothesis: Warmer water temperatures will increase the respiration rate of fish.

Respiration Rate of Guppies (Breaths per minute)

Temperature of Water	Trial #1 Respiration Rate	Trial #2 Respiration Rate	Trial #3 Respiration Rate	Trial #4 Respiration Rate	Average (Mean)
20°C	78	78	77	79	78
24°C	120	124	122	126	123
26°C	170	180	161	177	172
28°C	201	202	203	202	202

Conclusion: _____

_____

_____

II.   Hypothesis: Greater air pressure will increase the height a basketball bounces.

Conclusion: _____

_____

_____

_____

_____

_____

Height of Ball Bounce

[Bar graph showing Average Height (cm) on the y-axis (0 to 200) and Air Pressure on the x-axis:
4 PSI = 53, 6 PSI = 67, 8 PSI = 125, 12 PSI = 173]

Scientific Measurement · Chapter 1

The International System (SI) of Measurement

Scientists throughout the world use the SI system of measurement. The standard units in SI are shown below.

Measurement	Definition	SI Unit	Symbol
length	the distance between two points	meter	m
volume	the measure of the amount of space an object occupies	cubic meter	m^3
mass	the measure of the amount of matter in an object	gram	g
weight	the measure of force	Newton	N
temperature	the measure of the amount of heat an object has	degrees Celsius	°C
time	the measure for the interval between two events	second	s
area	the measure of the number of square units needed to cover the faces or surfaces of a figure	square meters	m^2

The Metric System is used to measure SI units.

Length	Mass	Capacity
1 centimeter = 10 millimeters 1 meter = 100 centimeters 1 kilometer = 1,000 meters	1 kilogram = 1,000 grams	1 liter = 1,000 milliliters
Abbreviations	**Abbreviations**	**Abbreviations**
1 millimeter = 1 mm 1 centimeter = 1 cm 1 meter = 1 m 1 kilometer = 1 km	1 milligram = 1 mg 1 gram = 1 g 1 kilogram = 1 kg	1 milliliter = 1 mL 1 liter = 1 L 1 kiloliter = 1 kL

SI Prefixes

Prefix	Meaning
kilo-	1,000
hecto-	100
deca-	10
unit	1
deci-	0.1
centi-	0.01
milli-	0.001

Using the Prefix Table

Adding a prefix to the unit of measurement changes its value.

Example:

kilo + meter = 1,000 meters
hecto + meter = 100 meters
deci + meter = 0.1 meter
centi + meter = 0.01 meter
milli + meter = 0.001 meter

Name: _____ Date: _____

Chapter 1   **Measurement—Applying Your Knowledge**

Sometimes scientists need to convert from one unit of measure to another similar unit. Converting from one unit to another involves using mathematical operations.

Example Problem 1: How many centimeters are there in 7 meters?	
Step 1: Write down the measurement you want to convert.	7 meters
Step 2: Write the conversion factor for the problem. The conversion factor is written as a fraction.	$7 \text{ m} \times \dfrac{100 \text{ cm}}{1 \text{ m}}$ units you are converting to / units you are converting from
Step 3: The units in the measurement you want to convert cancel out the units in the denominator of the fraction.	$7 \text{ m} \times \dfrac{100 \text{ cm}}{1 \text{ m}}$
Step 4: Multiply the measurement you want to convert by the fraction.	$7 \times \dfrac{100}{1} = \dfrac{700}{1} = 700 \text{ cm}$
Example Problem 2: 50 centimeters equal how many meters?	
Step 1: Write down the measurement you want to convert.	50 centimeters
Step 2: Write the conversion factor for the problem. The conversion factor is written as a fraction.	$50 \text{ cm} \times \dfrac{1 \text{ m}}{100 \text{ cm}}$ units you are converting to / units you are converting from
Step 3: The units in the measurement you want to convert cancel out the units in the denominator of the fraction.	$50 \text{ cm} \times \dfrac{1 \text{ m}}{100 \text{ cm}}$
Step 4: Multiply the measurement you want to convert by the fraction.	$50 \times \dfrac{1}{100} = \dfrac{50}{100} = 0.5 \text{ m}$

I. Complete the problems.

1. 48 L = _____ mL
2. 88 kg = _____ g
3. 108 g = _____ kg
4. 12 cm = _____ mm
5. 14 m = _____ cm
6. 6.25 L = _____ mL
7. 6 mL = _____ L
8. 9.5 m = _____ cm
9. 3 m = _____ cm
10. 1,500 mL = _____ L

II. Circle the appropriate unit to measure capacity.

1. bathtub   mL   L
2. drinking cup   mL   L

III. Circle the appropriate unit to measure length.

1. apple seed   mm   cm   m
2. earthworm   mm   cm   m
3. whale   mm   cm   m

IV. Circle the appropriate unit to measure mass.

1. bowling ball   g   kg
2. pine cone   g   kg

Microscopes

A microscope is used to help magnify the features of objects. The microscope most often used in middle school classrooms is the compound microscope. A compound microscope has two or more lenses.

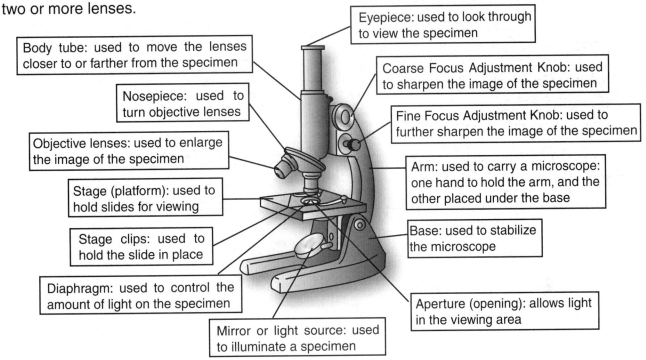

Eyepiece: used to look through to view the specimen

Body tube: used to move the lenses closer to or farther from the specimen

Coarse Focus Adjustment Knob: used to sharpen the image of the specimen

Nosepiece: used to turn objective lenses

Fine Focus Adjustment Knob: used to further sharpen the image of the specimen

Objective lenses: used to enlarge the image of the specimen

Arm: used to carry a microscope: one hand to hold the arm, and the other placed under the base

Stage (platform): used to hold slides for viewing

Stage clips: used to hold the slide in place

Base: used to stabilize the microscope

Diaphragm: used to control the amount of light on the specimen

Aperture (opening): allows light in the viewing area

Mirror or light source: used to illuminate a specimen

How to Use a Microscope

Step #1: Place the microscope on a table or flat surface with the arm facing you.

Step #2: Turn the coarse focus knob to raise the objective lenses above the stage.

Step #3: Turn the nosepiece until the lower-power objective lens locks into position.

Step #4: Look through the eyepiece. Adjust the light source and the diaphragm so that the field of view (the area you see) is bright.

Step #5: Fasten your slide to the microscope stage using the stage clips. Move the slide around until your specimen is centered in your field of view.

Step #6: Turn the coarse focus knob to lower the objective lens.

Step #7: Look through the eyepiece. Slowly, turn the coarse adjustment knob until you see the specimen. You may have to move the slide on the stage until the specimen is in the field of view.

Step #8: Use the diaphragm to adjust how much light is hitting the field of view.

Step #9: Turn the fine adjustment knob to sharpen the focus. If you need more magnification, turn the nosepiece until the high-power objective locks into place. Focus using the fine focus adjustment knob. Adjust the diaphragm.

Remember

(1) **Never** lower the objective lens while looking through the eyepiece. Instead, watch from the side while you turn the focus knob. If the lens hits the slide, both the lens and the slide may break.

(2) **Do Not** let direct sunlight strike a microscope mirror. You could damage your eyes.

Name: _____   Date: _____

Microscopes—Applying Your Knowledge

I.   Label the parts of a compound microscope.

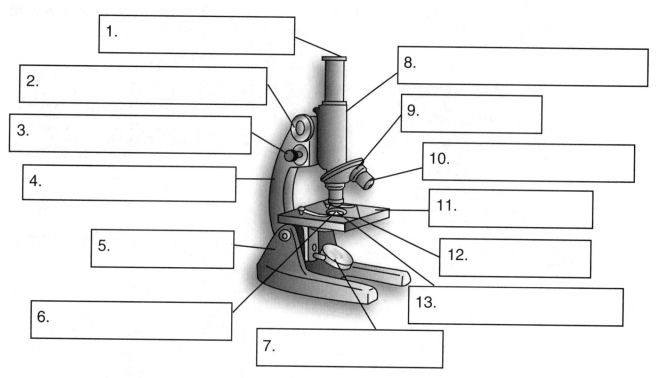

1.

2.

3.

4.

5.

6.

7.

8.

9.

10.

11.

12.

13.

II.   Match the microscope part with its function (the job it does).

_____ 1. adjustment knobs

_____ 2. arm

_____ 3. base

_____ 4. light source

_____ 5. eyepiece

_____ 6. stage platform

_____ 7. objective lenses

_____ 8. stage clip

_____ 9. diaphragm

a. used to look through to view the specimen
b. used to enlarge the image of the specimen
c. used to hold slides for viewing
d. used in carrying a microscope
e. used to bring the image into focus
f.   used to illuminate a specimen; consists of a bulb or mirror
g. used to hold the slide in place
h. used to control the amount of light on the specimen
i.   used to stabilize the microscope

Metric Rulers

Metric rulers or meter sticks are used to measure the height, length, or width of an object. They are also used to measure the distance between two objects or distance traveled by an object. Metric rulers deal with centimeters (cm) and millimeters (mm) only.

The larger lines with numbers are centimeters. The smaller lines are millimeters.

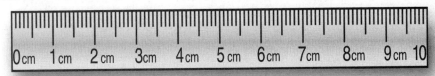

A ruler starts on 0.

Reading Metric Measurements

The metric system is based on the number 10 and multiples of 10. There are 10 mm in 1 cm, or a millimeter is 0.1 (1/10th) of a centimeter.

Example: If you measure 3 small marks after the 7-centimeter mark, it is 7.3 cm (centimeters) long, which is 73 mm (millimeters).

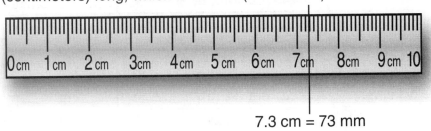

7.3 cm = 73 mm

Measuring with a Metric Ruler

Step #1: Place the zero end of your ruler at the end of the object being measured. Make sure the end of the ruler is even with your object. Use your left hand to hold the ruler in place.

The snail is 2.7 cm long.

Step #2: Look to the opposite side of the object you are measuring. Read the last number on your ruler that is below the object. This will indicate the length of the object in centimeters. Then count the number of small marks the object measures beyond the last centimeter. This is the number of millimeters.

2 centimeters + 7 millimeters = 2.7 cm or 27 mm

Name: _____ Date: _____

Chapter 1   Metric Rulers—Applying Your Knowledge

I.   Record the length that corresponds to each line along the metric ruler. Label your answers in centimeters.

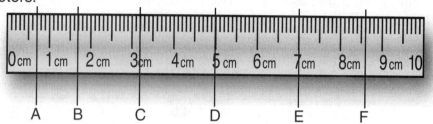

A. _____   B. _____   C. _____
D. _____   E. _____   F. _____

II. Once you are familiar with metric measurements, you should be a good judge of the approximate size of things. With a partner, estimate and then measure the following objects. Record the answers in the data table below.

Object	Estimate	Measurement
1. length of your pencil	___ cm ___ mm	___ cm ___ mm
2. width of your science book	___ cm ___ mm	___ cm ___ mm
3. height of the classroom door	___ cm ___ mm ___ m	___ cm ___ mm ___ m
4. length of the classroom	___ cm ___ mm ___ m	___ cm ___ mm ___ m
5. length of your shoe	___ cm ___ mm	___ cm ___ mm

III. Would you use millimeters, centimeters, meters, or kilometers to measure the following lengths? Circle the most sensible metric unit of measure.

1.	length of an apple seed	mm	cm	m	km
2.	length of an earthworm	mm	cm	m	km
3.	height of a telephone pole	mm	cm	m	km
4.	length of a basketball court	mm	cm	m	km
5.	width of Lake Erie	mm	cm	m	km
6.	width of a ladybug	mm	cm	m	km
7.	height of the Empire State Building	mm	cm	m	km
8.	length of a staple	mm	cm	m	km
9.	height of a tree	mm	cm	m	km
10.	width of a pencil	mm	cm	m	km
11.	distance from Texas to Indiana	mm	cm	m	km

Graduated Cylinders

Types of Graduated Cylinders

Liquid volume is measured using a graduated cylinder. The metric unit used is milliliter (mL). Graduated cylinders come in a variety of sizes including 10 mL, 25 mL, 50 mL, 100 mL, 500 mL, and 1,000 mL.

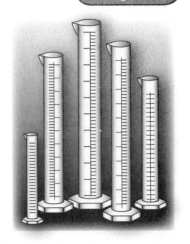

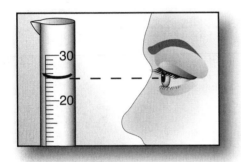

Reading a Graduated Cylinder

Place the graduated cylinder on a flat surface such as a table or counter top. Your eyes should be directly level with the liquid. The liquid will tend to curve downward. This curve is called the **meniscus**. Read the volume at the bottom of the meniscus.

Calibration of a Graduated Cylinder

A graduated cylinder is calibrated. This means that the cylinder is divided or marked with lines forming a scale. The lines are the same distance apart from one mark to the next. There are a variety of scales used to label graduated cylinders. It is important to determine the scale (increments or value of each mark on the scale) before using it.

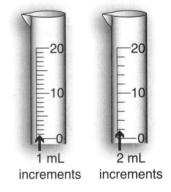

1 mL
increments

2 mL
increments

Measuring With a Graduated Cylinder

Read the volume at the bottom or lowest point of the meniscus. If the volume is between two marks on the scale, record the reading using a decimal.

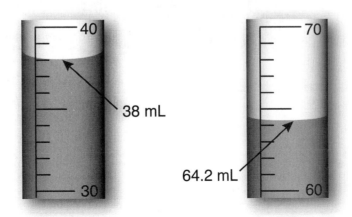

38 mL

64.2 mL

Name: _____ Date: _____

Chapter 1 **Graduated Cylinders—Applying Your Knowledge**

I. Determine the scale for each graduated cylinder.

 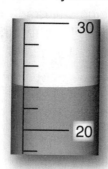 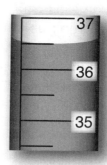

a. _____   b. _____   c. _____

II. Draw in the meniscus for the following readings.

a. 35 mL   b. 8 mL   c. 19 mL   d. 2.5 mL

III. Determine the volume of the liquids in the following cylinders.

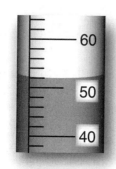 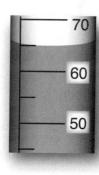 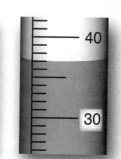 

a. _____   b. _____   c. _____   d. _____

Balance Scales

A laboratory balance is used to measure the mass of an object. Mass is recorded in units such as kilograms (kg), grams (g), or milligrams (mg). There are several different balances that can be used to measure mass.

Double-Pan Balance

A double-pan balance has a pan or platform on each side of the balance. This type of balance measures mass by comparing the mass of an object to standard known masses placed on the opposite pan.

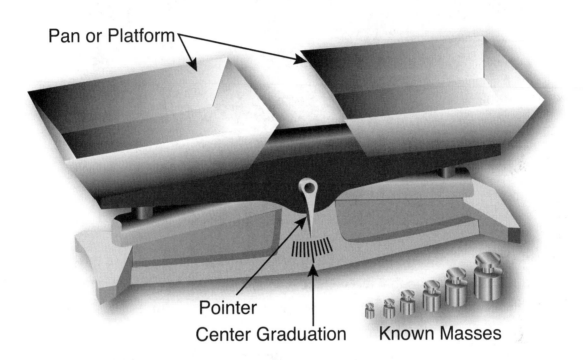

Pan or Platform

Pointer
Center Graduation   Known Masses

How to Use a Double-Pan Balance

Step #1:   Set the balance on a table or level surface.

Step #2:   Make sure both pans of the balance are clean and empty.

Step #3:   Line the pointer up with the center graduation. (Use the adjustment knob on the back of the balance to make the pan even.)

Step #4:   Place the object to be weighed in one pan. The pointer will swing to the opposite side.

Step #5:   Place masses in the other pan until the pointer is again lined up with the center graduation.

Step #6:   Add up the values printed on each weight placed in the pan. The total is equal to the mass of the object.

Chapter 1   # Balance Scales (cont.)

Triple-Beam Balance

On one side of the balance is a pan (or platform) on which you place the object to be measured. On the other side are three beams. Each beam has a sliding weight called a rider. One beam might be marked in intervals of 10 grams, the second in 100 grams, and the third in tenths (0.1) of a gram.

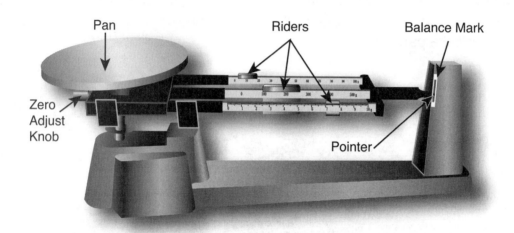

How to Use a Triple-Beam Balance

Step #1:   Set the balance on a table or level surface.

Step #2:   Slide all riders back to the zero point. Make sure the riders rest in the notches in the beams. Check to see that the pointer swings freely along the scale. The beam should swing an equal distance above and below the zero point. If it does not, you must calibrate or "zero the balance." Turn the zero adjustment screw until the line on the pointer comes to rest at the zero mark on the scale. Repeat this procedure to "zero the balance" every time you use it.

Step #3:   Place the object to be measured on the pan. The pointer will rise.

Step #4:   Move the largest rider along its beam until the pointer drops below the zero mark on the scale. When this happens, back the rider up one notch. Repeat the procedure with the next-sized rider.

Sept #5:   Slide the smallest rider along its beam. If the rider causes the pointer to drop below the zero mark, begin sliding it in the opposite direction. Continue sliding the rider back and forth until the pointer lines up exactly with the zero mark on the scale.

Step #6:   Find the mass by adding the measurements on the riders. Remember: If you are measuring the mass of something in a container, (1) find the mass of the empty container, (2) find the mass of the container plus the substance you want to measure, and (3) subtract the two masses. The difference is the mass of the substance.

Name: _____   Date: _____

Balance Scales—Applying Your Knowledge   Chapter 1

I.   Determine the mass in grams of each object.

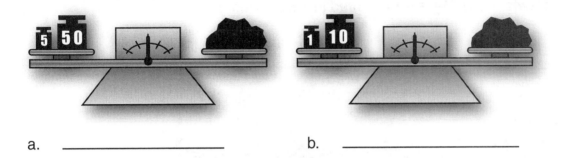

a. _____   b. _____

II.   The mass indicated on the triple-beam balance below is _____ grams.

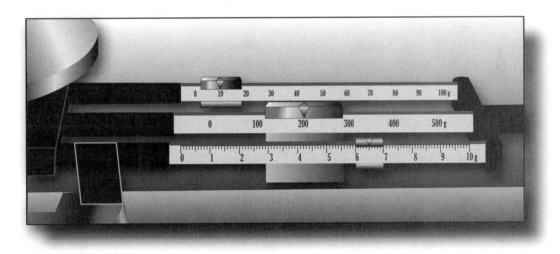

III.   Fill different film canisters with various objects such as pennies, paper clips, popcorn, screws, or washers that will get you closest to the targeted mass. Now, measure the mass of each canister using a balance scale. Record your answers in the data table below.

Target Mass (g)	Items Used	Actual Mass (g)
9 grams		
15 grams		
110 grams		
200 grams		
250 grams		
325 grams		
467 grams		

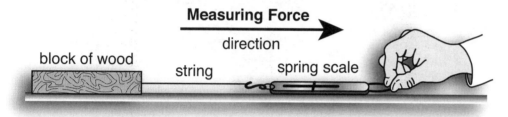

Chapter 1

Spring Scales

A spring scale can be used to measure both the amount of force needed to move an object over a given distance and the mass of the object being moved. Force is measured in units called Newtons (N). Mass is measured in units called grams (g).

Measuring Force

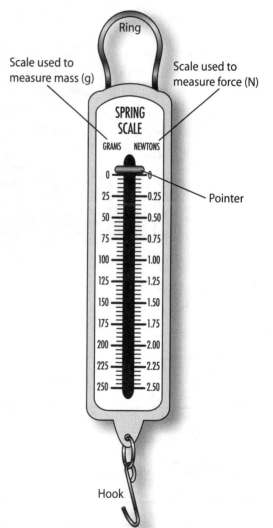

How to Use a Spring Scale

<u>Vertically</u> (⟨↕⟩)

Step #1:   Attach the spring scale to the object being measured. (Usually, one end of a string is tied to the spring scale hook, and the other end is tied to or around the object being measured.)

Step #2:   Rest the object on a flat surface.

Step #3:   Without pulling the object up, read the units of force while the object is resting on the flat surface.

Step #4:   Gently pull up on the spring scale until the object is completely lifted off the desk.

Step #5:   Read the units of force required to lift or move the object.

Step #6:   Record the measurement in Newtons (N).

<u>Horizontally</u> (⟵⟶)

Step #1:   Attach the spring scale to the object being measured. (Usually, one end of a string is tied to the spring scale hook, and the other end is tied to or around the object being measured.)

Step #2:   Rest the object on a flat surface.

Step #3:   Without pulling the object, read the units of force while the object is at rest.

Step #4:   Pull the object across the table with the spring scale.

Step #5:   Read the units of force required to move the object.

Step #6:   Record the measurement in Newtons (N).

Name: _____ Date: _____

Spring Scales—Applying Your Knowledge Chapter 1

I.   Draw the pointer for each of the following readings.

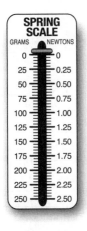   

a.   2.00 N   b.   0.75 N   c.   2.50 N   d.   1.00 N

II. Practice using a spring scale. Collect and clean an empty milk carton from the school cafeteria. Tie a string around the carton and connect it to a spring scale. First, pull the carton across the table. Record how much force it took to move the empty carton across the table in the data table below. Next, fill the carton with marbles. Use the spring scale to pull the carton across the table. Record your answer below.

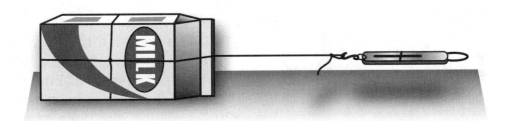

Carton	Force in Newtons (N)
1. empty carton	
2. full carton	

Chapter 1   # Thermometers

Temperature is expressed in degrees (°). The Fahrenheit (°F) and Celsius (°C), or centigrade, temperature scales are the two most common scales used in science classrooms and on thermometers.

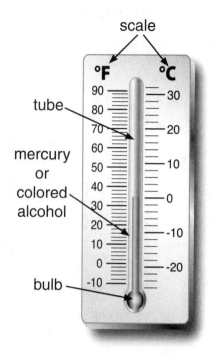

A thermometer is calibrated. This means that the tube is divided or marked with lines. The lines are the same distance apart from one mark to the next. Both scales (Fahrenheit and Celsius) are divided in two-degree increments.

Thermometers are commonly made of glass. The bulb is connected to a tube with a numbered scale written on the outside. Inside the glass tube is a liquid like mercury or colored alcohol that rises and falls in the tube as the temperature around it warms or cools.

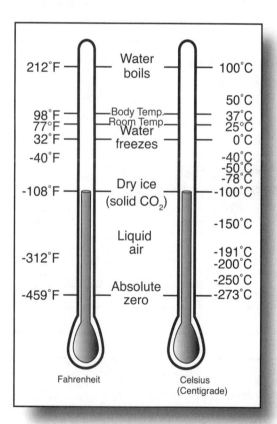

Most thermometers have both the Fahrenheit and Celsius scales. If you know the temperature on one scale, you can read across to tell the temperature on the other scale.

How to Use a Thermometer

Step #1: When you read the temperature on a thermometer, it should be held vertically, and your eyes should be level with the top of the liquid in the glass tube.

Step #2: When you take your readings, avoid handling the bulb or tube of the thermometer. The heat from your hands will transfer to the glass, causing the temperature to change.

Step #3: When using a thermometer outside, place it away from buildings and put it in the shade. Keep the thermometer out of snow and rain.

Name: _____ Date: _____

Thermometers—Applying Your Knowledge Chapter 1

I.   Use the thermometer on page 26 to complete the data table.

	Fahrenheit	Celsius
1. water boils		
2. body temperature		
3. room temperature		
4. water freezes		

II. Read the directions and record your answers on the thermometers below.

1. Color in the mercury bar to 0 degrees Celsius on thermometer #1.
    What is the temperature in degrees Fahrenheit? _____

2. Color in the mercury bar to 50 degrees Fahrenheit on thermometer #2.
    What is the temperature in degrees Celsius? _____

3. Color in the mercury bar to 20 degrees Fahrenheit on thermometer #3.
    What is the temperature in degrees Celsius? _____

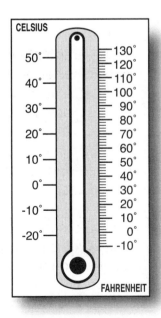

Thermometer #1

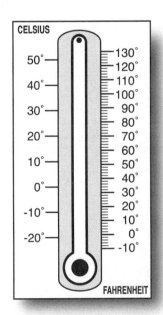

Thermometer #2

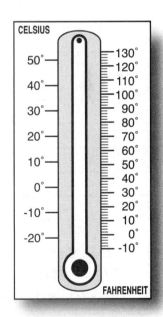

Thermometer #3

Name: _____ Date: _____

Chapter 2 Water Temperature and Surface Tension

Water molecules form bonds that hold them together. The one oxygen and two hydrogen atoms of a water molecule are held together because they share electrons: this is called a **covalent bond**. Water molecules are attracted to each other because of a force called **cohesion**. As the molecules cling to each other, they form an invisible "skin" on the surface of the water or what scientists call **surface tension**. Surface tension helps a drop of water hold its shape, to hang on to itself, and stack up on a surface. It also helps some insects walk on the surface of the water. Let's find out how water temperature affects surface tension.

Step #1: PURPOSE
Write a question that asks what you want to learn from the investigation.

Purpose: Does temperature affect the number of drops needed for surface tension on a penny?

Step #2: RESEARCH
Investigate the chemistry of water, surface tension, and cohesion.

_____

_____

_____

_____

_____

_____

_____

_____

_____

 Check It Out! Learn more about surface tension at the following animated web site. "Surface Tension." University of Florida.
<http://citt.ufl.edu/Marcela/Sepulveda/html/en_tension.htm>

Step #3: HYPOTHESIS
Write a sentence that predicts what your investigation will prove.

_____

_____

Name: _____ Date: _____

Materials
1 penny
eyedropper
200 mL of room-temperature water
200 mL of hot water
paper towels

Variables
Independent: water temperature
Dependent: number of water drops on top of the penny
Constants: same penny, same side of the penny, same size water drops

Experiment
Controlled Setup
Step 1:   Place the penny on a flat surface. (Use the same side of the penny for both the Controlled and Experimental parts of the experiment.)
Step 2:   Using the room-temperature water, carefully add one drop of water at a time onto the surface of the penny.
Step 3:   Count the number of drops added to the surface before the water spills over the edge of the penny.
Step 4:   Dry the penny and repeat Steps 1–3 four times.

Troubleshooting
Practice filling and using the eyedropper before beginning the experiment.

Experimental Setup
Step 1:   Place the penny on a flat surface.
Step 2:   Using hot water, carefully add one drop of water at a time onto the surface of the penny.
Step 3:   Count the number of drops added to the surface before the water spills over the edge of the penny.
Step 4:   Dry the penny and repeat Steps 1–3 four times.

Results
Record the number of drops added to the penny for each trial in the data table below. Calculate and record the average for each group.

Control Group Drops						
Temperature	**Trial #1**	**Trial #2**	**Trial #3**	**Trial #4**	**Trial #5**	**Average**
Room Temperature						

Experimental Group Drops						
Temperature	**Trial #1**	**Trial #2**	**Trial #3**	**Trial #4**	**Trial #5**	**Average**
Hot Water						

Name: _____ Date: _____

Create a graph that will compare the average number of drops added to the penny in the control group with the experimental group. Place the dependent variable (number of drops) on the *y*-axis. Place the independent variables (room-temperature water and hot water) on the *x*-axis.

Water Temperature and Surface Tension

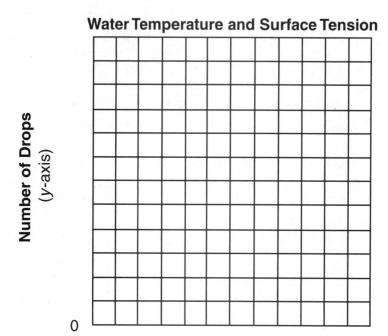

Number of Drops
(*y*-axis)

0

(*x*-axis)
Water Temperature

_____

_____

_____

_____

_____

_____

_____

Name: _____ Date: _____

Calcium and Bones

Our body needs **calcium** to build strong, healthy teeth and bones. During childhood and adolescence, bones grow the most. It is important to get enough calcium during these years. The more **bone mass** accumulated early in life, the less likely one would be to develop a serious bone problem. Low calcium levels can increase the likelihood of broken bones, unhealthy teeth, and even a disease called rickets. As an adult, low levels of calcium can cause osteoporosis, a painful condition caused by the decrease in bone density (the amount of calcium) in bones. The elderly may experience broken hips and other fractures with decreased bone density.

Building and maintaining strong bones depends on the mineral calcium. Without it, your bones would be bendable and would not be able to support your body. While many foods contain calcium, dairy products are the most significant source. Let's find out what happens when minerals are removed from bones.

Step #1: PURPOSE
Write a question that asks what you want to learn from the investigation.

Purpose: Does the amount of vinegar affect the mass of a chicken bone?

Step #2: RESEARCH
Investigate vinegar as an acid, calcium, calcium carbonate, and how calcium relates to bone mass and density.

_____

_____

_____

_____

_____

_____

Check It Out! Learn more about calcium and the importance of building strong bones at the following interactive web site. "Milk Matters." National Institutes of Health. <http://www.nichd.nih.gov/milk/milk.cfm>

Step #3: HYPOTHESIS
Write a sentence that predicts what your investigation will prove.

_____

_____

Name: _____ Date: _____

Step #4: PROCEDURE
Plan and carry out the investigation. This includes gathering the materials, identifying the variables, following the step-by-step directions, and recording the data.

Materials
4 cooked chicken bones
triple-beam balance
4 jars with lids

50 mL of distilled water
225 mL of white vinegar
Distilled water for rinsing

Variables
Independent: amount of vinegar
Dependent: mass of bone
Constants: same type of bone, same amount of solution, time in solution

Experiment
Controlled Setup
Step 1:   Rinse off one chicken bone with distilled water until all meat is removed.
Step 2:   Measure the bone's mass using a triple-beam balance. Record the measurement in the data table.
Step 3:   Place one bone in a jar filled with 50 mL of distilled water. Tighten the lid and let stand for three days.
Step 4:   After three days, remove the bone from the jar and measure its mass.
Step 5:   Record the measurement in the data table.

Troubleshooting
Make sure the bones are completely submerged in the liquid solutions.

Experimental Setup
Step 1:   Rinse one chicken bone with distilled water until meat is removed.
Step 2:   Measure the bone's mass using a triple-beam balance. Record the measurement in the data table.
Step 3:   Place the bone in a jar filled with 50 mL of vinegar. Tighten the lid and let stand for three days.
Step 4:   After three days, remove the bone from the jar and measure its mass.
Step 5:   Record the measurement in the data table.
Step 6:   Repeat Steps 1–5 two times using 75 mL and 100 mL of vinegar.

Results
Use a triple-beam balance scale to measure the beginning and ending bone mass. Record the measurements in the data table below.

Control Group		
Amount of Water	**Beginning Mass**	**Ending Mass**
Experimental Group		
Amount of Vinegar	**Beginning Mass**	**Ending Mass**

Name: _____ Date: _____

Step #5: ANALYSIS
Study the results of your experiment. Decide what the data means. This information can then be used to help you draw a conclusion about what you learned in your investigation.

Create a graph that will compare using water in the control group with using different amounts of vinegar in the experimental group. Place the dependent variable (mass) on the y-axis. Place the independent variable (amount of vinegar) on the x-axis.

Affects of Vinegar on Mass

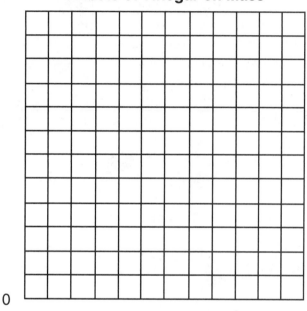

Bone Mass (g)
(y-axis)

0

(x-axis)
Amount of Vinegar (mL)

Step #6: CONCLUSION
Write a summary of the experiment (what actually happened). It should include the purpose, a brief description of the procedure, and whether or not the hypothesis was supported by the data collected.

_____

_____

_____

_____

_____

_____

_____

Name: _____ Date: _____

Chapter 2   # Mass and Speed

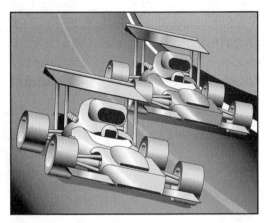

Winning the Indy 500 depends on many factors, including the speed at which the race car can perform. Car designers and engineers understand the relationship between mass and speed and use this knowledge to create cars to help drivers win the race.

In the 1600s, the scientist **Isaac Newton** studied motion. He discovered a relationship between **mass** and **inertia** (the tendency of objects to resist a change in motion). These ideas became Newton's first law of motion. Understanding this law can help engineers improve the performance of race cars. They know changing the mass of a race car can cause a change in **speed** (the distance the vehicle will travel in a certain amount of time), and speed is the key to winning at the Indianapolis Motor Speedway. Let's find out how mass affects the speed of an object.

Step #1: PURPOSE
Write a question that asks what you want to learn from the investigation.

Purpose: Does mass affect the speed of a toy car rolling down a ramp?

Step #2: RESEARCH
Investigate Newton's Laws of Motion, speed, mass, and inertia.

_____

_____

_____

_____

_____

_____

_____

_____

Check It Out! Learn more about Newton's Laws of Motion at the following web site. "Newton's Laws of Motion." Florida Space Research Institute. <http://www.steelbeach.com/fsri/PropulsionTheory/01NewtonsLaws/PT-01-005.shtml>

Step #3: HYPOTHESIS
Write a sentence that predicts what your investigation will prove.

_____

_____

Name: _____ Date: _____

Step #4: PROCEDURE
Plan and carry out the investigation. This includes gathering the materials, identifying the variables, following the step-by-step directions, and recording the data.

Materials

toy car   stopwatch
triple-beam balance   meter stick
3 books   3 pennies
ramp (at least 1 meter long)
tape   calculator

Variables
Independent: mass
Dependent: speed
Constants: same toy car, same ramp height

Experiment
Controlled Setup

Step 1: Find the mass of the car and record it in the data table.
Step 2: Stack the three books on the floor. Place one end of the ramp on the books and the other on the floor.
Step 3: Place the rear wheels of the car at the top end of the ramp.
Step 4: Release the car as you start the stopwatch.
Step 5: Stop timing when the front of the car gets to the bottom of the ramp. Record the time in the data table.
Step 6: Calculate the speed of your car by using the formula: $speed = \dfrac{distance}{time}$
Step 7: Repeat steps 3–6 two more times.

Troubleshooting
Practice using a stopwatch before doing the experiment.

Experimental Setup

Step 1: Tape the pennies on top of the car. Find the mass and record in the data table.
Step 2: Place the rear wheels of car at the top end of the ramp.
Step 3: Release the car as you start the stopwatch.
Step 4: Stop timing when the front of the car gets to the bottom of the ramp. Record the time in the data sheet.
Step 5: Calculate the speed and record in the data table.
Step 6: Repeat steps 2–5 two more times.

Results

Record the mass, time, and distance. Calculate the speed for each trial. Then calculate the average speed for each group and record in the data table below.

	Control Group Car (No Pennies)				Experimental Group Car (3 Pennies)			
Trial	Mass (g)	Distance (cm)	Time (s)	Speed (cm/s)	Mass (g)	Distance (cm)	Time (s)	Speed (cm/s)
#1								
#2								
#3								
Average Speed: _____					Average Speed: _____			

Name: _____ Date: _____

Step #5: ANALYSIS
Study the results of your experiment. Decide what the data means. This information can then be used to help you draw a conclusion about what you learned in your investigation.

Create a graph that will compare the mass and the average speed of the toy car in the control group with the mass and average speed of the toy car in the experimental group. Place the dependent variable (average speed of the cars) on the *y*-axis. Place the independent variables (mass of the control car and experimental car) on the *x*-axis.

Mass and Speed

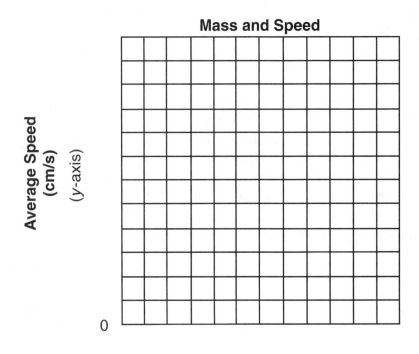

Average Speed (cm/s) (*y*-axis)

0

(*x*-axis)
Car Mass (g)

Step #6: CONCLUSION
Write a summary of the experiment (what actually happened). It should include the purpose, a brief description of the procedure, and whether or not the hypothesis was supported by the data collected.

_____

_____

_____

_____

_____

_____

_____

Name: _____ Date: _____

Temperature and Elasticity

Chapter 2

Bungee jumping is an extreme sport based on the two types of mechanical energy: potential and kinetic. Standing on the platform, ready to dive, the jumper has **potential energy** (stored energy ready to be used). As the person free falls, the potential energy changes to **kinetic energy** (energy in motion). After falling for the length of the cord, elastic potential energy comes into play. The cord acts like a spring. The cord allows the jumper to free fall toward the earth and then be snatched back up before hitting the ground.

Elastic potential energy is the energy stored in elastic materials as the result of their stretching or compressing. Elastic potential energy can be stored in rubber bands, trampolines, springs, a drawn bow with arrow, and bungee cords. Let's see how temperature can affect elasticity.

Step #1: PURPOSE
Write a question that asks what you want to learn from the investigation.

Purpose: Does the temperature of a rubber band affect the distance it will stretch?

Step #2: RESEARCH
Investigate elastic potential energy, rubber, and force.

_____

_____

_____

_____

_____

_____

_____

Check It Out! Learn more about elastic potential energy at the following web site. "How The Crossbow Works." How Stuff Works, Inc. <http://science.howstuffworks.com/crossbow1.htm>

Step #3: HYPOTHESIS
Write a sentence that predicts what your investigation will prove.

_____

_____

Name: _____ Date: _____

Materials
10 rubber bands, the same size   masking tape
2 wooden clothespins   meter stick

> **Variables**
> *Independent:* temperature
> *Dependent:* distance the
>   rubber band stretches
> *Constants:* same size rubber
>   bands, same clothespins

Experiment
Controlled Setup
Step 1:   Secure a meter stick to the floor with tape.
Step 2:   Starting at "0," lay one room-temperature rubber band on the floor alongside the meter stick.
Step 3:   Have your partner grasp one end of the rubber band with a wooden clothespin.
Step 4:   Grasp the other end of the rubber band with a wooden clothespin. Stretch the rubber band along the meter stick until it breaks.
Step 5:   Record the distance stretched in the data table.
Step 6:   Repeat procedure with the other four room-temperature rubber bands.

> **Troubleshooting**
> A spring scale can be used, but be careful as it may not be strong enough for the amount of force needed to stretch the rubber band, and it could break.

Experimental Setup
Step 1:   Place five rubber bands in the freezer for 15 minutes (Keep in the freezer until each is needed).
Step 2:   Starting at "0," lay one frozen rubber band on the floor alongside the meter stick.
Step 3:   Have your partner grasp one end of the rubber band with a wooden clothespin.
Step 4:   Grasp the other end of the rubber band with a wooden clothespin. Stretch the rubber band along the meter stick until it breaks.
Step 5:   Record the distance stretched in the data table.
Step 6:   Repeat procedure with the other four frozen rubber bands.

Results
Record the distance each rubber band was stretched until broken in the data table below. Calculate and record the average for each group.

Control Group					
Temperature	**Trial #1**	**Trial #2**	**Trial #3**	**Trial #4**	**Trial #5**	**Average**
Room Temperature						

Experimental Group					
Temperature	**Trial #1**	**Trial #2**	**Trial #3**	**Trial #4**	**Trial #5**	**Average**
Frozen						

Name: _____ Date: _____

Step #5: ANALYSIS
Study the results of your experiment. Decide what the data means. This information can then be used to help you draw a conclusion about what you learned in your investigation.

Create a graph that will compare the average distance the rubber band was stretched in the control group with the average distance the rubber band was stretched in the experimental group. Place the dependent variable (distance) on the y-axis. Place the independent variable (temperature) on the x-axis.

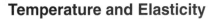

Temperature and Elasticity

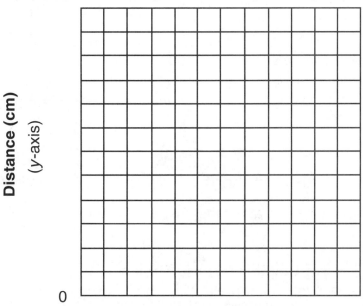

Distance (cm) (y-axis)

0

(x-axis)
Temperature

Step #6: CONCLUSION
Write a summary of the experiment (what actually happened). It should include the purpose, a brief description of the procedure, and whether or not the hypothesis was supported by the data collected.

_____

_____

_____

_____

_____

_____

_____

Name: _____ Date: _____

Chapter 2   Ultraviolet Light and Sunscreen

Light travels in the form of electromagnetic waves. There are many different types of electromagnetic waves, most of which cannot be detected by the human eye. The full range of electromagnetic waves is called the **electromagnetic spectrum**. The only part of the electromagnetic spectrum that you can see with your eyes is visible light.

Ultraviolet (UV) light is one of the invisible frequencies of light that is given off by the sun. The sun emits ultraviolet radiation, which travels in the form of electromagnetic waves. Overexposure to it can be harmful. Its effects can be seen as sunburn on the skin. Sunscreen helps prevent sunburn caused by UV radiation. All sunscreen lotions have an SPF (Sun Protection Factor) value that correlates with its UV protection. Let's find out how the SPF in a sunscreen affects the amount of UV rays absorbed by a substance.

Step #1: PURPOSE
Write a question that asks what you want to learn from the investigation.

Purpose: Does the SPF in a sunscreen affect the amount of UV radiation absorbed by a UV detecting bead?

Step #2: RESEARCH
Investigate electromagnetic spectrum, ultraviolet radiation, sunscreen SPF, and UV beads.

_____

_____

_____

_____

_____

_____

_____

_____

Check It Out! Learn more about the electromagnetic spectrum at the following web site. "The Electromagnetic Light Spectrum." National Aeronautics and Space Administration. <http://science.hq.nasa.gov/kids/imagers/ems/visible.html>

Step #3: HYPOTHESIS
Write a sentence that predicts what your scientific investigation will prove.

_____

_____

Name: _____ Date: _____

Step #4: PROCEDURE

Plan and carry out the investigation. This includes gathering the materials, identifying the variables, following the step-by-step directions, and recording the data.

Materials
1 package of UV detecting beads
3 sunscreen lotions with SPF values of 15, 30, and 45
4 medium zip-top baggies

Experiment
<u>Controlled Setup</u>

Step 1: Divide the package of UV beads equally into the 4 zip-top baggies.

Step 2: Label one bag "No sunscreen". This bag will not be coated with sunscreen and will automatically be rated a "5" in the data chart for showing the most dramatic color change.

<u>Experimental Setup</u>

Step 1: Coat one baggie with 10 mL of sunscreen and label with the SPF value.

Step 2: Repeat Step 1 for the other two baggies and the other two sunscreens.

Step 3: Place the baggies from the Control Setup and Experimental Setup outdoors in direct sunlight.

Step 4: Allow the beads to absorb UV rays for 15 minutes.

Step 5: Rate the bead color on a scale of 1–5, with 5 showing the most dramatic color change or "burning" and 1 showing the least color change.

	Variables
	Independent: SPF number
	Dependent: color of beads
	Constants: number of beads, size of baggie, amount of light, amount of sunscreen

	Troubleshooting
	Do not use sunscreen if it is past its expiration date.

Results
Rate the bead color on a scale of 1–5, with 5 showing the most color or "burning" and 1 showing the least color. Record the ratings in the data table below.

	Control Group	Experimental Group		
SPF Number	**None**	**15**	**30**	**45**
Rating (1–5)				

Name: _____ Date: _____

Create a graph that will compare the bag of UV beads without sunscreen in the control group with the bags of UV beads with sunscreen in the experimental group. Place the dependent variable (rating of UV bead color) on the *y*-axis. Place the independent variable (SPF value) on the *x*-axis.

Ultraviolet Rays and Sunscreen

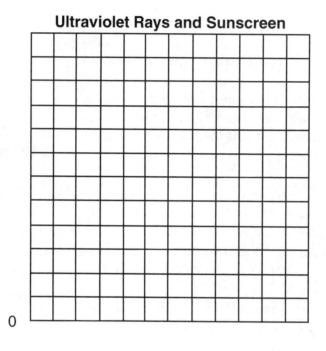

Color Rating (1–5)
(*y*-axis)

0

(*x*-axis)
SPF Value

_____

_____

_____

_____

_____

_____

_____

Name: _____ Date: _____

Electricity and Lemon Power

Electricity is the flow of **electrons**. One kind of electric current, direct current, can be found in a single-cell device called a **battery**. The **direct current** (DC) in a battery produces electricity in a circuit that **moves in only one direction**. A battery stores chemical energy and makes it available in an electrical form.

A lemon can be used to make a battery. The lemon battery is called a **voltaic battery** because it changes chemical energy into electrical energy. The lemon battery can be made by pushing two different metals (copper and zinc) into a lemon. These metals act like the electrodes in a real battery. The acid in the lemon operates as an electrolyte (the liquid that conducts electricity in a battery). The electrodes lose and gain electrons from each other, producing electricity. Touching the electrodes to your tongue closes the circuit and allows a small electric current to flow. Let's find out how a lemon can produce enough electricity to tickle your tongue.

Step #1: PURPOSE
Write a question that asks what you want to learn from the investigation.

Purpose: Does the gauge of a wire affect the amount of electrical current a lemon can produce?

Step #2: RESEARCH
Investigate electricity, electrons, electrodes, electrolytes, parts of a battery, and voltaic battery.

_____

_____

_____

_____

_____

_____

_____

_____

Check It Out! Learn more about electricity at the following interactive web site. "Electricity and Magnetism." U.S. Department of Energy. <http://ippex.pppl.gov/interactive/electricity/intro.html>

Step #3: HYPOTHESIS
Write a sentence that predicts what your investigation will prove.

_____

_____

Name: _____ Date: _____

Materials

3 cm bare 10-gauge copper wire
3 cm bare 12-gauge copper wire
3 cm bare 18-gauge copper wire
sheet of coarse sandpaper

3 cm strip of zinc
medium-sized lemon
wire clippers

Variables
Independent: gauge of wire
Dependent: tingle effect
Constants: same lemon, same zinc strip

Experiment

Controlled Setup

Step 1: Smooth any rough spots on the ends of the wires and piece of zinc with sandpaper.

Step 2: Gently roll the lemon on a flat surface using a little pressure to "squeeze" or soften the lemon. Don't rupture the skin of the lemon.

Step 3: Push the piece of zinc and 18-gauge wire into the lemon so they are as close together as possible without touching.

Step 4: Moisten your tongue with saliva. Touch the tip of your wet tongue to the free ends of the zinc strip and copper wire.

Step 5: Record the amount of current or "tingle" you felt on your tongue on a scale of 1–10 (1 being a slight tingle; 10 being a strong tingle) in the data table.

Step 6: Remove the 18-gauge wire. Leave the zinc strip in the lemon.

Experimental Setup

Step 1: Repeat steps 3–6 using the 12-gauge and 10-gauge wires. Place the wires in the same hole each time.

Troubleshooting

1. When placing the wire into the lemon, it must be as close to the zinc as possible without touching.
2. Lemons only produce a tiny amount of voltage. The amount depends on the acidity of the lemon. Try using a voltmeter if you doubt the lemon is producing any voltage.
3. Make sure the lemon is rolled until softened.
4. You need lots of saliva on your tongue before touching it to the wires.

Results

Record the amount of current or "tingle" you felt on your tongue on a scale of 1–10 (1 being a slight tingle; 10 being a strong tingle) in the data table.

	Control Group	Experimental Group	
Wire Gauge	18	12	10
Tingle Effect (1–10)			

Name: _____ Date: _____

Create a graph that will compare the wire gauge and the amount of tingle created in the control group with the wire gauge and amount of tingle created in the experimental group. Place the dependent variable (tingle effect 1–10) on the *y*-axis. Place the independent variables (gauges of wire) on the *x*-axis.

Wire Gauge Effect on Lemon Electric Current

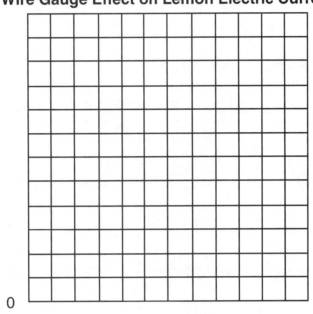

0

(*x*-axis)
Gauge of Wire

_____

_____

_____

_____

_____

_____

_____

Name: _____   Date: _____

Light and Seed Germination

Germination is the growth of an embryonic (developing) plant contained within a seed. Flowering plants reproduce by forming seeds. Seeds have three parts: **seed coat** (protects the new plant inside the seed), **embryo** (new plant), and the **cotyledon** (seed leaves). Most seeds go through a period where there is no active growth. During this time, the seed can be safely transported to a new location. Under favorable conditions, the seed begins to germinate, and the embryo develops into a seedling.

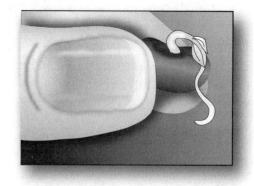

The germination of seeds is dependent on both internal and external conditions. Moisture content of the seed is an important internal factor in seed germination. Important external factors include light, temperature, and water. When conditions are right, the seed opens, and the embryo emerges. Let's find out how light affects the germination time of a radish plant.

Step #1: PURPOSE
Write a question that asks what you want to learn from the investigation.

Purpose: Does the color of light affect the germination time of a radish seed?

Step #2: RESEARCH
Investigate germination, external conditions of a radish seed, and monocot seeds.

_____

_____

_____

_____

_____

_____

_____

_____

 Check It Out! Learn more about seed germination at the following interactive web site. "Life Cycle of a Seed Plant." Teachers' Domain. <http://www.teachersdomain.org/resource/lsps07.sci.life.stru.seedplant/ >

Step #3: HYPOTHESIS
Write a sentence that predicts what your investigation will prove.

_____

_____

Name: _____ Date: _____

Step #4: PROCEDURE
Plan and carry out the investigation. This includes gathering the materials, identifying the variables, following the step-by-step directions, and recording the data.

Materials
5 small shallow boxes
1 package of radish seeds
water
paper towels

clear plastic wrap
aluminum foil
red, blue, green cellophane
*enough of each wrapping
material to cover a box

Variables
Independent: color of light
Dependent: germination time
Constants: same type of seed,
   same amount of water,
   same amount of sunlight
   exposure, same number of
   seeds in each box

Experiment
Controlled Setup
Step 1:   Fold and moisten several layers of paper towels to fit the bottom of the box.
Step 2:   Place 8–10 radish seeds on the wet paper towels.
Step 3:   Cover the box with clear plastic wrap.
Step 4:   Place the box near a sunny window and observe daily for germination.
Step 5:   Record the number of days required for seed germination in the data table.

Troubleshooting
Be sure to keep seeds moist, or they will not germinate properly.

Experimental Setup
Step 1:   Fold and moisten several layers of paper towels to fit in the bottom of the remaining boxes.
Step 2:   Place 8–10 radish seeds on the wet paper towels in each box.
Step 3:   Cover one box in aluminum foil. Cover each of the 3 remaining boxes in a different colored cellophane: red, blue, and green.
Step 4:   Place the boxes near a sunny window, and observe daily for germination.
Step 5:   Record the number of days required for germination to begin for each box.

Results
Record the number of days required for germination to begin for each box in the table below.

Control Group							
Color of Light	**Day 1**	**Day 2**	**Day 3**	**Day 4**	**Day 5**	**Day 6**	**Day 7**
Natural							
Experimental Group							
Color of Light	**Day 1**	**Day 2**	**Day 3**	**Day 4**	**Day 5**	**Day 6**	**Day 7**
Red							
Blue							
Green							
Foil (no light)							

Name: _____   Date: _____

Create a graph that will compare the seeds getting normal light in the control group with the seeds getting colored or no light in the experimental group. Place the dependent variable (time) on the *y*-axis. Place the independent variable (color of light) on the *x*-axis.

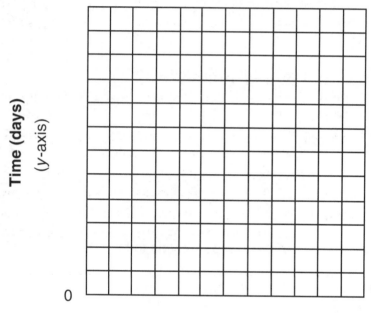

Affects of Light Color on Seed Germination

Time (days)
(*y*-axis)

0

(*x*-axis)
Color of Light

_____

_____

_____

_____

_____

_____

Name: _____ Date: _____

Fertilizer and Petunias

Plants make their own food by a process called **photosynthesis**. They take energy from the sun, carbon dioxide from the air, and water and nutrients (chemical elements) from the soil. In order for a plant to grow and thrive, it needs a number of different chemical elements. Nitrogen, phosphorus, and potassium are the most important of these **elements**. Many gardeners use commercially manufactured fertilizer, because they contain these elements. Let's find out how plants grown with commercial fertilizers compare with those grown without fertilizer.

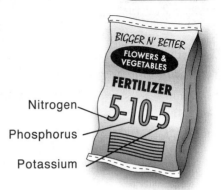

Step #1: PURPOSE
Write a question that asks what you want to learn from the investigation.

Purpose: Does the amount of fertilizer affect the growth rate of a petunia plant?

Step #2: RESEARCH
Investigate the ingredients in fertilizers, the effects of fertilizer on plants, and fertilizing recommendations. Research petunia plants and the climate and soil they thrive in and the amount of water needed for normal growth rate and photosynthesis.

_____

_____

_____

_____

_____

_____

_____

_____

_____

Check It Out! Learn more about photosynthesis at the following animated web site. "Illuminating Photosynthesis." Public Broadcasting Service. <http://www.pbs.org/wgbh/nova/methuselah/photosynthesis.html>

Step #3: HYPOTHESIS
Write a sentence that predicts what your investigation will prove.

_____

_____

Name: _____ Date: _____

Materials

6 petunia plants (same size)
6 identical pots   1 bag potting soil
  water   metric ruler
  fertilizer (such as Miracle Gro™)

Variables
Independent: fertilizer
Dependent: height
Constants: water, sunlight, soil type, size of pot, same growing environment, plant type

Experiment

Controlled Setup

Step 1:   Label three pots "A." Number each pot. Measure equal amounts of soil into each of the pots. Plant a petunia in each pot. Give each plant 100 mL of water.

Step 2:   Give each plant 100 mL of water once a week for 8 weeks.

Experimental Setup

Step 1:   Label three pots "B." Number each pot. Measure equal amounts of soil into each of the pots. Plant a petunia in each pot.

Step 2:   Give each plant 100 mL of water once a week for 8 weeks.

Step 3:   Give each plant 25 mL of premixed fertilizer every two weeks.

Troubleshooting

1. Measure the height of the main plant from the border of the container to the top of the main plant stem. Do not measure from the top of the soil, as the soil may condense with watering over time.
2. Make sure pots have holes in the bottom to allow the roots to "breathe" and for excess water to drain out.
3. Mix fertilizer according to package directions.
4. Place the 6 plants near a sunny window or under a grow light.

Results

Measure and water the plants on the same day of the week for 8 weeks. Record height measurements in centimeters in the data table and calculate the average growth rate.

Week	Height of Plants in Control Group				Height of Plants in Experimental Group			
	#1	#2	#3	Average	#1	#2	#3	Average
#1								
#2								
#3								
#4								
#5								
#6								
#7								
#8								

Name: _____ Date: _____

Step #5: ANALYSIS
Study the results of your experiment. Decide what the data means. This information can then be used to help you draw a conclusion about what you learned in your investigation.

Create a graph that will compare the average growth rate of petunias in the control group with the average growth rate of petunias in the experimental group. Place the dependent variable (height) on the y-axis. Place the independent variables (plants) on the x-axis.

Affect of Fertilizer on Plant Growth

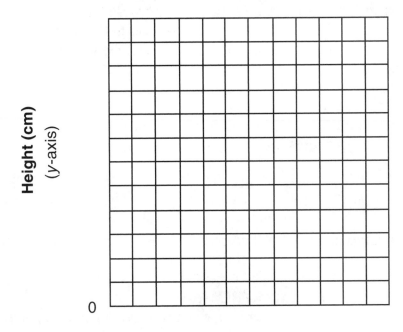

Height (cm)
(y-axis)

0

(x-axis)
Plants

Step #6: CONCLUSION
Write a summary of the experiment (what actually happened). It should include the purpose, a brief description of the procedure, and whether or not the hypothesis was supported by the data collected.

_____

_____

_____

_____

_____

_____

_____

Name: _____ Date: _____

 # DNA Extraction and Onions

Scientists studied cells for many years before they discovered how **traits** (characteristics) of parents were passed on to their offspring. By the end of the nineteenth century, scientists had learned the secret code of **heredity** (passing physical and character traits from one generation to another). **Chromosomes** (rod-shaped strands containing genetic material) located in the nucleus of the cell are made up of genes. The genes consist of a long strand of DNA. The **DNA** contains the **genetic blueprint** (code) for how an organism looks and functions. The substances in the DNA are arranged in a three-dimensional structure that looks like a ladder. DNA is used in the judicial courts to prove or disprove family relationships, identify missing persons, and identify criminals and victims in criminal activities.

Onions are a good sample to use in DNA extraction because they have very little starch in them. To get DNA out of the cell, you need to break open the cell; detergent can be used to burst the cell membrane and let the DNA float out of the cell. Let's find out how soap affects the DNA extraction from an onion.

Step #1: PURPOSE
Write a question that asks what you want to learn from the investigation.

Purpose: Does the type of soap used in the DNA extraction from an onion affect the amount of DNA extracted?

Step #2: RESEARCH
Investigate DNA structure of an onion, parts of a plant cell, chromosome location in a cell, and DNA's use in the court systems.

_____

_____

_____

_____

_____

Check It Out! Learn more about DNA at the following interactive web site. "Using Genomics: DNA Detectives." Canadian Museum of Nature. <http://nature.ca/genome/03/d/40/03d_40_e.cfm>

Step #3: HYPOTHESIS
Write a sentence that predicts what your investigation will prove.

_____

_____

Name: _____ Date: _____

Step #4: PROCEDURE
Plan and carry out the investigation. This includes gathering the materials, identifying the variables, following the step-by-step directions, and recording the data.

Materials

10 g non-iodized salt
blender   coffee filters
2 g meat tenderizer
30 mL liquid dish soap
30 mL Murphy's Vegetable Oil Soap™
4 small beakers
glass stirring rod

500 g chopped onion
funnel
60 mL warm water
200 mL rubbing alcohol

microscope and slides

Variables
Independent: type of soap used in extraction
Dependent: DNA extraction
Constants: same amount of soap

Experiment

Controlled Setup

Step 1: Blend 250 g chopped onions, 30 mL warm water, and 5 g salt. Pour the mixture into a beaker.

Step 2: Add 30 mL liquid dish soap and stir gently for 5 minutes.

Troubleshooting
Be sure to use the correct amount of water in the mixture (buffer), as DNA will dissolve in water.

Step 3: Pour the mixture into the filtered funnel. Filter out all the liquid into another beaker.

Step 4: Add 1 g meat tenderizer to the liquid.

Step 5: Measure the filtered liquid.

Step 6: Add an equal amount of rubbing alcohol to the mixture. The alcohol will form a separate layer on top of the onion mixture.

Step 7: The white strings floating to the top are strands of DNA. Gently stir the alcohol layer.

Step 8: Use the stirring rod to remove a white DNA string and place on a microscope slide. View through a microscope and sketch observations below.

Experimental Setup

Step 1: Repeat steps in the controlled setup using the Murphy's Vegetable Oil Soap™ instead of liquid dish soap.

Results

Record your observations. Sketch the DNA extraction from the control and experimental groups.

Control Group Sketch	Experimental Group Sketch

Name: _____ Date: _____

Step #5: ANALYSIS

Study the results of your experiment. Decide what the data means. This information can then be used to help you draw a conclusion about what you learned in your investigation.

Use the Venn diagram below to compare and contrast your observations of the control with the experimental results of the DNA extraction.

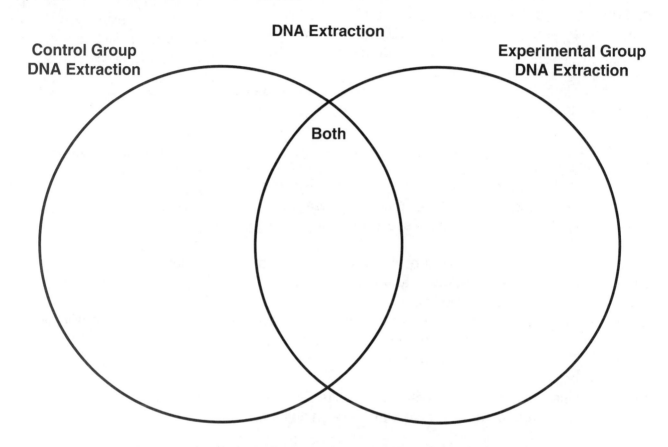

DNA Extraction

**Control Group
DNA Extraction**

Both

**Experimental Group
DNA Extraction**

Step #6: CONCLUSION

Write a summary of the experiment (what actually happened). It should include the purpose, a brief description of the procedure, and whether or not the hypothesis was supported by the data collected.

_____

_____

_____

_____

_____

_____

Name: _____ Date: _____

pH and Soil

Soil is a valuable natural resource. Life on earth depends on the soil. Plants are rooted in the soil and obtain nutrients from it for growth. Animals eat plants or other animals that eat plants.

There are many different types of soil, and each one has unique characteristics. Most soils contain four basic components: mineral particles, water, air, and organic matter that comes from decaying, dead plants and animals. The kinds of soils in an area help determine how well crops grow there. Soil can be acid, alkaline or neutral. Highly acidic or alkaline soils can harm many plants.

The term **pH** refers to the acidity or alkalinity of a substance. The pH scale ranges from 0 to 14. Testing the soil using a pH-testing kit can determine its condition (pH of 1 to 6 is acidic; pH 7 is neutral; and pH of 8 to 14 is alkaline). Most plants grow best within a **pH range** of 6.5 to 7.2. Changing the pH of a soil is frequently required to grow healthy plants. Let's find out how the pH level of soil can be affected by adding a neutral substance to it.

Step #1: PURPOSE
Write a question that asks what you want to learn from the investigation.

Purpose: Does the pH level of the water in soil affect the root of a coleus plant?

Step #2: RESEARCH
Investigate the pH levels, composition, and formation of different types of soils.

_____

_____

_____

_____

_____

_____

_____

 Check It Out! Learn more about soil at the following interactive web site.
"The Dirt on Soil". Discovery Education.
<http://school.discoveryeducation.com/schooladventures/soil/>

Step #3: HYPOTHESIS
Write a sentence that predicts what your scientific investigation will prove.

_____

_____

Name: _____ Date: _____

Step #4: PROCEDURE

Plan and carry out the investigation. This includes gathering the materials, identifying the variables, following the step-by-step directions, and recording the data.

Materials

6 coleus plants (same size)
6 identical pots with hole
  in bottom
2 beakers
baking soda

eye dropper
metric ruler
glass stirring rod
distilled water

litmus paper and pH chart
graduated cylinder for measuring
1 bag potting soil
white vinegar

Experiment

Controlled Setup

Step 1: Label three pots "A." Number

Variables
Independent: pH level of water
Dependent: height of plant
Constants: plant type and size, sunlight, soil type, size of pots, same growing environment

Troubleshooting
Measure the height of the main plant stem from the border of the container to the top of the main plant stem.

each pot. Measure equal amounts of soil into each of the pots. Plant a coleus plant in each pot. Measure and record the beginning height of each plant.

Step 2: Pour 300 mL of distilled water into one of the beakers. Use litmus paper and a litmus pH chart to measure the pH level of the water in the neutral or control beaker. It should be 7.0. If it is higher, add a drop or two of vinegar, stir, and check it again. If it is lower than 7.0, sprinkle in a pinch of baking soda, stir, and check the pH again. Repeat until the color scale shows that the pH level is 7.0. Give each plant 100 mL of this water. Repeat Step 2 each week for four weeks.

Experimental Setup

Step 1: Label three pots "B." Number each pot. Measure equal amounts of soil into each of the pots. Plant a coleus plant in each pot. Measure and record the beginning height of each plant.

Step 2: Pour 300 mL of distilled water into the other beaker. Pour 15 mL of vinegar into the beaker, stir, and check the pH level. It should be 4.0. If it is higher or lower, add vinegar or baking soda as in Step 2 of the Controlled Setup to reach 4.0. Give each plant 100 mL of this water. Repeat Step 2 each week for four weeks.

Step 3: Place all six plants near a sunny window or under a grow light.

Results

Measure and water the plants on the same day for four weeks. Record measurements in centimeters in the data table and calculate the average growth rate.

Week	Height of Control Group A				Height of Experimental Group B			
	Plant #1	Plant #2	Plant #3	Average	Plant #1	Plant #2	Plant #3	Average
Beginning								
Week 1								
Week 2								
Week 3								
Week 4								

Name: _____ Date: _____

Step #5: ANALYSIS
Study the results of your experiment. Decide what the data means. This information can then be used to help you draw a conclusion about what you learned in your investigation.

Create a bar graph that will compare the average growth rate of the coleus plants in the control group with the average growth rate of the coleus plants in the experimental group. Place the dependent variable (average height) on the *y*-axis. Place the independent variables (pH level of watering solution for control and experimental group) on the *x*-axis.

Affect of pH on Plant Growth

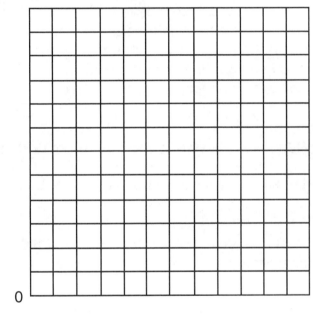

Average Height (cm)
(*y*-axis)

0

(*x*-axis)
pH Level of Watering Solution

Step #6: CONCLUSION
Write a summary of the experiment (what actually happened). It should include the purpose, a brief description of the procedure, and whether or not the hypothesis was supported by the data collected.

_____

_____

_____

_____

_____

_____

_____

Name: _____ Date: _____

 **Salinity and Brine Shrimp**

Brine shrimp or Sea-Monkeys™ are **crustaceans** that live in salt marshes, mangrove swamps, and **tidal flats**. The **salinity** or salt level of these waters is very high. Brine shrimp are unique animals because they thrive in salty water. They prefer water that is just as or slightly saltier than the oceans, but they can survive in water that is many times saltier.

One of the things that make brine shrimp fascinating is their ability to lay eggs called cysts. If you put brine shrimp cysts in salt water, they hatch very quickly, and the shrimp mature in about eight days. Brine shrimp are an importance food source for fish and crustaceans raised in home aquariums. Let's find out how salinity affects the hatching of brine shrimp eggs.

Step #1: PURPOSE
Write a question that asks what you want to learn from the investigation.

Purpose: Does the amount of salt in water affect the hatching of brine shrimp?

Step #2: RESEARCH
Investigate hatching and growing brine shrimp, salinity, cysts, and salt (NaCl).

_____

_____

_____

_____

_____

_____

_____

Check It Out! Learn more about brine shrimp at the following web site.
"Brine Shrimp and the Ecology of the Great Salt Lakes." U.S. Department of the Interior.
<http://ut.water.usgs.gov/shrimp/index.html>

Step #3: HYPOTHESIS
Write a sentence that predicts what your investigation will prove.

_____

_____

Name: _____ Date: _____

Step #4: PROCEDURE
Plan and carry out the investigation. This includes gathering the materials, identifying the variables, following the step-by-step directions, and recording the data.

Materials
200 brine shrimp eggs (sold at pet stores)
60 g sea salt or non-iodized salt
4 clear glass containers (label containers with the amount of salt added)
1 L room-temperature water (bottled or aged tap water)

Variables
Independent: amount of salt
Dependent: number of brine shrimp hatched
Constants: same number of eggs in the water, same amount of water, same temperature of water

Experiment
Controlled Setup
Step 1:   Pour 250 mL of room-temperature bottled water into a glass container.
Step 2:   Sprinkle 50 brine shrimp eggs onto the surface of the water.
Step 3:   Place container in direct sunlight or under a grow light.
Step 4:   Count the number of eggs hatched after 24 hours and record in the data table.

Troubleshooting
The brine shrimp should start hatching in just 24 hours. They will live 1–3 days without food. To feed the brine shrimp and keep them alive longer, add a pinch of yeast. (Too much yeast can kill the shrimp).

Experimental Setup
Step 1:   Pour 250 mL of room-temperature bottled water into a glass container.
Step 2:   Add 10 g of sea salt and mix.
Step 3:   Sprinkle 50 brine shrimp eggs over the surface of the water.
Step 4:   In the third container, mix 20 g salt with 250 mL water, and in the last container, mix 30 g salt with 250 mL water.
Step 5:   Place 50 brine shrimp eggs in each container.
Step 6:   Count the number of eggs hatched after 24 hours in each container and record in the data table.

Results
Count the number of eggs hatched after 24 hours and record in the data table.

Control Group	
Amount of Salt (g)	**Number of Eggs Hatched**
0 g	
Experimental Group	
Amount of Salt (g)	**Number of Eggs Hatched**
10 g	
20 g	
30 g	

Oceanography: Salinity and Brine Shrimp

Step #5: ANALYSIS
Study the results of your experiment. Decide what the data means. This information can then be used to help you draw a conclusion about what you learned in your investigations.

Create a graph that will compare the number of eggs hatched in the control group with the number of eggs hatched in the experimental group. Place the dependent variable (number of eggs hatched) on the *y*-axis. Place the independent variable (amount of salt) on the *x*-axis.

Brine Shrimp and Salt Water

Number of Eggs Hatched (*y*-axis)

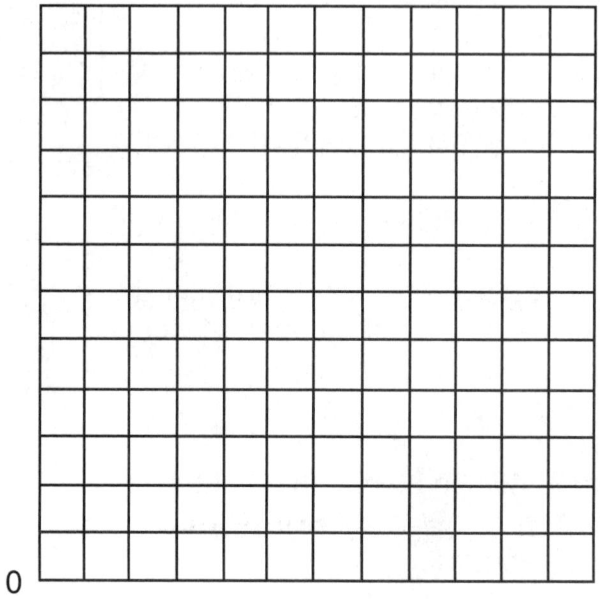

0

(*x*-axis)
Amount of Salt (g)

Step #6: CONCLUSION
Write a summary of the experiment (what actually happened). It should include the purpose, a brief description of the procedure, and whether or not the hypothesis was supported by the data collected.

_____

_____

_____

_____

_____

_____

_____

Name: _____ Date: _____

Temperature and Greenhouse Effect   Chapter 4

The Earth's atmosphere (or air) is a layer of gases such as water vapor, carbon dioxide, nitrous oxide, and methane surrounding the planet. The Earth's atmosphere regulates the climate. It acts like a giant blanket covering the earth, trapping the gases and heating up the surface. Scientists call this phenomenon the **greenhouse effect**.

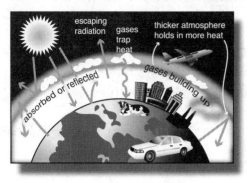

The greenhouse effect is nature's heating system. Without it, life on Earth would not be possible; it would be too cold. Sunlight enters the Earth's atmosphere, passing through the blanket of greenhouse gases. As it reaches the Earth's surface, the sunlight's energy is absorbed. Once absorbed, this energy is released back into the atmosphere. Some of the energy passes back into space, but much of it remains trapped in the atmosphere by the gases, causing our world to heat up.

In recent years, there has been concern about the rise of global temperatures. Many scientists believe this temperature increase is due to an increased use of fossil fuels. The gases formed by the burning fossil fuels, such as carbon dioxide, are building up in the atmosphere. They act like the greenhouse gases and trap heat energy inside the atmosphere of Earth. The result, some scientists believe, is that the Earth is heating up and undergoing **global warming**, which is changing our climate. Let's find out how the greenhouse effect increases water temperature.

Step #1: PURPOSE
Write a question that asks what you want to learn from the investigation.

Purpose: Does a covered jar affect the temperature of water in the jar?

Step #2: RESEARCH
Investigate fossil fuels, greenhouse effect, global warming, and Earth's changing climate.

_____

_____

_____

_____

Check It Out! Learn more about the greenhouse effect at the following animated web site.
"Greenhouse Effect." Scripps Institution of Oceanography.
<http://earthguide.ucsd.edu/earthguide/diagrams/greenhouse/>

Step #3: HYPOTHESIS
Write a sentence that predicts what your investigation will prove.

_____

_____

Name: _____ Date: _____

Step #4: PROCEDURE
Plan and carry out the investigation. This includes gathering the materials, identifying the variables, following the step-by-step directions, and recording the data.

Materials
2 identical glass jars
500 mL water, room temperature
2 thermometers
1 zip-top baggie (large enough to cover jar)

Experiment

Controlled Setup
Step 1:   Pour 250 mL of water into a glass jar.
Step 2:   Place a thermometer into the water.
Step 3:   Record the water temperature in the data table.
Step 4:   Place the jar (with the thermometer in it) in direct sunlight or under a heat source.
Step 5:   After two hours, record the water temperature in the data table.

Experimental Setup
Step 1:   Pour 250 mL of water into a glass jar.
Step 2:   Place a thermometer into the water.
Step 3:   Record the water temperature in the data table.
Step 4:   Place the jar (with the thermometer in it) in a zip-top baggie and close. (This will create the greenhouse effect.)
Step 5:   Place the jar in direct sunlight or under a heat source.
Step 6:   After two hours, record the water temperature in the data table.

> **Variables**
> Independent: covered/uncovered glass
> Dependent: water temperature
> Constants: same amount of water, same amount of heat exposure, same type of jar

> **Troubleshooting**
> 1. Make sure the baggie on the greenhouse jar is securely zipped.
> 2. Make sure you can read the thermometer's scale through the jar and baggie.

Results
Record the beginning temperatures and ending temperatures of both the control and experimental groups in the data table below. Calculate the difference in temperatures and record the answers in the data table.

Control Group			
Glass Jar	**Starting Temperature**	**Ending Temperature**	**Difference**
Uncovered Jar			

Experimental Group			
Glass Jar	**Starting Temperature**	**Ending Temperature**	**Difference**
Covered Jar			

Name: _____ Date: _____

Step #5: ANALYSIS
Study the results of your experiment. Decide what the data means. This information can then be used to help you draw a conclusion about what you learned in your investigation.

Create a graph that will compare the difference in temperatures in the control group with the difference in temperatures in the experimental group. Place the dependent variable (difference in temperatures) on the *y*-axis. Place the independent variables (covered glass, uncovered glass) on the *x*-axis.

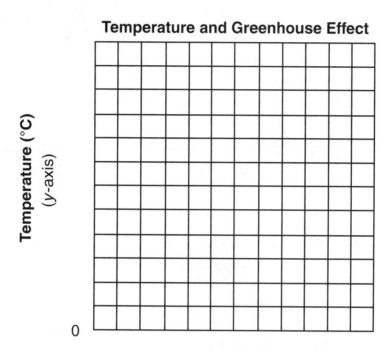

Temperature and Greenhouse Effect

Temperature (°C) (*y*-axis)

0

(*x*-axis)
Uncovered and Covered Jars

Step #6: CONCLUSION
Write a summary of the experiment (what actually happened). It should include the purpose, a brief description of the procedure, and whether or not the hypothesis was supported by the data collected.

_____

_____

_____

_____

_____

_____

Name: _____ Date: _____

Chapter 4   # Mass and Impact Craters

While several theories exist as to the formation of the moon, one of the most popular assumes that a large unknown object struck the earth many years ago, blasting material way from the earth. This material was captured in the earth's gravitational orbit. Pieces of this debris collided with each other, causing enough heat to melt and fuse the particles together, eventually forming the moon.

The landscape of the moon is not like Earth's. If you look at the moon with a telescope, you will see that its surface is covered with different-sized holes known as **impact craters**. Impact craters are the remains of collisions between the moon and asteroids, comets, or meteorites. Because the moon has no atmosphere, wind, or water to cause erosion, the moon's features remain unchanged through time.

Since its initial formation, the moon has been bombarded by millions of pieces of space debris to create the cratered surface that is now observed on the moon. There are three factors that affect the size of a crater—**mass**, **speed**, and **size** of the impacting debris. Let's find out if a difference in mass affects the size of an impact crater.

Step #1: PURPOSE
Write a question that asks what you want to learn from the investigation.

Purpose: Does the mass of a marble affect the size of an impact crater?

Step #2: RESEARCH
Investigate impact craters, meteors, meteorites, and gravitational force of the moon.

_____

_____

_____

_____

_____

Check It Out! Learn more about the moon at the following web site.
"Lunar and Planetary Science: The Moon." National Aeronautics and Space Administration.
<http://nssdc.gsfc.nasa.gov/planetary/planets/moonpage.html>

Step #3: HYPOTHESIS
Write a sentence that predicts what your scientific investigation will prove.

_____

_____

Name: _____ Date: _____

Step #4: PROCEDURE
Plan and carry out the investigation. This includes gathering the materials, identifying the variables, following the step-by-step directions, and recording the data.

Materials

triple-beam balance   masses
large tray 10–15 cm deep   flour
sand to fill tray about 8 cm deep   metric ruler
3 marbles (different masses)

Variables
Independent: mass of marble
Dependent: size of impact crater
Constants: dropped from same
     height, depth of landing surface

Experiment

Controlled Setup

Step 1:   Measure the mass of each marble using the triple-beam balance. Record the measurements in the data table below.

Troubleshooting
Place newspaper on the floor under the sand tray to make clean-up easier.

Step 2:   Place the tray on the floor. Fill the tray with sand (8 cm deep).
Step 3:   Sprinkle a thin layer of flour over the sand.
Step 4:   Drop the marble with the medium mass into the sand from a height of 100 cm.
Step 5:   Remove the marble. Measure and record the width of the crater.
Step 6:   Smooth the sand out with the metric ruler and sprinkle a thin layer of flour over the sand.
Step 7:   Perform three trials with this marble. Record the average diameter of the crater.

Experimental Setup

Step 1:   Repeat steps 2–7 using the marbles with the smallest and largest masses.

Results

Record the mass of each marble and the width of the crater in the data table. Calculate and record the average diameter of the craters in the data table.

Controlled Setup				
Mass of Marble	**Trial #1 Diameter**	**Trial #2 Diameter**	**Trial #3 Diameter**	**Average**
Experimental Setup				
Mass of Marble	**Trial #1 Diameter**	**Trial #2 Diameter**	**Trial #1 Diameter**	**Average**

Name: _____ Date: _____

Study the results of your experiment. Decide what the data means. This information can then be used to help you draw a conclusion about what you learned in your investigations.

Create a graph that will compare the average diameter of the crater in the control group with the average diameter of the craters in the experimental group. Place the dependent variable (average diameter of crater) on the *y*-axis. Place the independent variable (mass of marble) on the *x*-axis.

Affect of Mass on Impact Craters

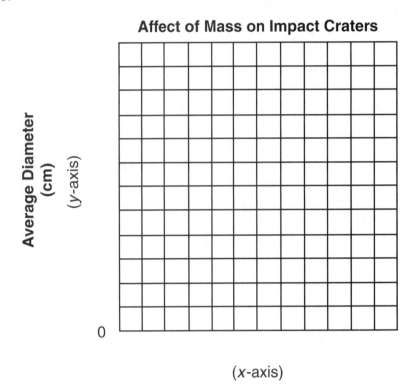

Average Diameter (cm) (*y*-axis)

0

(*x*-axis)
Mass of Marble (g)

Write a summary of the experiment (what actually happened). It should include the purpose, a brief description of the procedure, and whether or not the hypothesis was supported by the data collected.

_____

_____

_____

_____

_____

_____

Science Fair Guidelines

Before starting a science fair project, make certain your idea or topic is acceptable. Carefully read your school's project guidelines. Your experiment should not involve illegal substances, hazardous devices, or in any way present a danger to you or others involved in your project. Many science fair guidelines forbid projects involving animals because of ethical issues.

Project Categories

After your idea has been approved, you will need to determine in which category to enter your project. The day of the fair you will place your display board in that section. Your project will be judged along with the other entries in that category. The most common categories are listed below.

Behavioral Science
Botany
Chemistry
Computer Science
Medicine and Health
Earth Science
Microbiology

Engineering
Environmental Science
Mathematics

Physics
Space Science
Zoology

Basic Exhibit Rules

For safety reasons, certain items are not allowed to be used or displayed at a science fair. (Check your school's guidelines.) Drawings, photos, diagrams, or models should be used instead.

Items Not Allowed

- living creatures (animals, plants, or microorganisms)
- any type of cultured growth, spoiled food, or molds
- human or animal tissues such as teeth, hair, nails, or dried animal bones
- taxidermy items, preserved animals, or embryos
- water, soil, dried plant matter, or waste material
- chemicals of any kind
- food (human or animal)
- sharp instruments such as syringes, needles, or pipettes
- poisons, drugs, or controlled substances
- explosives, hazardous devices, or weapons; open flames, combustible materials, or containers (full or empty) used to store these substances

Name: _____ Date: _____

Science Fair Project Planner

Step #1: Choose a Topic
A good topic is one that can be tested with an experiment. It is important that your topic be one that interests you.

Topic: _____
_____
_____
_____

Step #2: Purpose
Write a question that asks what you want to learn from the project. Remember: (1) It should be clearly written, (2) it usually starts with the verb "Does," and (3) it can be answered by measuring something.

Purpose: _____
_____
_____
_____

Step #3: Research
The goal of the research is to find information that will help you make a prediction about what will occur in your experiment. First, identify the key words in your purpose. Next, look up each key word in an encyclopedia, dictionary, or textbook. Finally, expand your research to the Internet.

_____
_____
_____
_____
_____
_____
_____
_____
_____
_____
_____
_____
_____
_____

Step #4: Hypothesis
Make an educated guess about what you think will happen in your project. Your hypothesis should be clearly written. It should answer the question stated in the purpose, be brief and to the point, and identify the independent and dependent variables.

Hypothesis: _____
_____

Name: _____ Date: _____

Step #5: Procedure

Write a plan for your experiment. The plan should include a list of the materials needed, step-by-step directions (written like a recipe) for conducting the experiment, and identification of the variables. Remember to use metric units.

Materials: (Be specific; include types, quantities, and sizes of materials.)

Step-by-step directions for the experiment:

Variables:

Step #6: Results

Conduct the experiment and record the results in a data table. Your table should include a title, with parts clearly labeled, units of measurement identified, and if appropriate, the average (mean) for different trials of the experiment should be recorded. You need at least three trials.

Title _____

Name: _____ Date: _____

Step #7: Analysis

Study the results of your experiment. Create a graph to display your data. The graph should include a title, be clearly labeled, and identify the units of measurement. Place the dependent variable data on the y-axis. Place the independent variable data on the x-axis.

Title _____

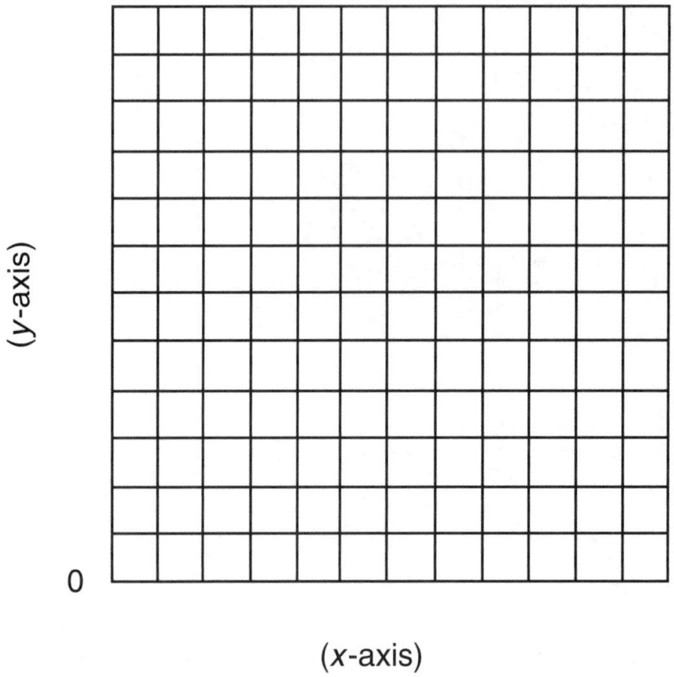

(y-axis)

0

(x-axis)

Step #8: Conclusion

Write a summary of the experiment (what actually happened). It should include the purpose, a brief description of the procedure, and whether or not the hypothesis was supported by the data collected. Use key facts from your research to help explain the results. The conclusion should be written in first person ("I").

_____
_____
_____
_____
_____
_____
_____
_____
_____
_____
_____
_____

Science Fair Exhibit

The exhibit is a visual way to communicate to others what you have learned from the investigation. Construct an exhibit using charts, graphs, photos, illustrations and/or diagrams of the experiment. This information is placed on a display board. The board has three sections and is usually made of cardboard or Styrofoam (check your school's guidelines for rules concerning the dimensions). The display should be neat, attractive, easy-to-read, colorful, and arranged in an orderly manner. It is important that you take the time to do a good job. The tools and materials used in the experiment may be displayed on the table in front of your board (if they are permitted).

Parts of an Exhibit
- **Purpose:** an explanation of what you wanted to find out (your question)
- **Hypothesis:** an educated guess as to what you thought would happen in your investigation
- **Materials:** a list of everything you needed to conduct the experiment
- **Procedure:** a step-by-step set of instructions detailing how the experiment was conducted, written in third person (no "I" or "you")
- **Variables:** a list of the independent, dependent, and controlled variables
- **Data:** the results of the experiment organized in a data table
- **Analysis:** the data organized in a graph, and an explanation of the results
- **Conclusion:** a summary of the experiment (what actually happened), it should include the purpose, a brief description of the procedure, and whether or not the hypothesis was supported by the data collected, written in first person ("I")
- **Abstract:** (not always required, so check your school's guidelines) a brief, written discussion of your science fair project, usually no more than one page, placed on the table in front of the display or attached to the board, written in first person ("I")

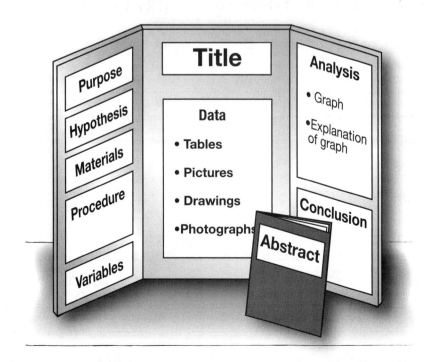

| Chapter 5 | **Science Fair Abstract** |

Each student who does a science fair project may be required to write an abstract that will be displayed with their project. An abstract is a brief, written report discussing the project. It may be written in first person. The abstract is printed on one page and is usually between 100 and 250 words in length (check your school's guidelines). The project's abstract may be placed on the table in a folder or attached to the display board.

An abstract consists of a brief statement of the most important information about your project. It should clearly and simply summarize the project. It should include the purpose, a brief description of the procedure, and whether or not the hypothesis was supported by the data collected. Spelling, grammar, punctuation, neatness, and originality are important. An abstract does not include a bibliography unless specifically required (check your school's guidelines).

Parts of an Abstract

<u>First Page</u>
Title Page: Center the project title, student's name, grade, and the name of the school, city, and state on the front page of the abstract.

<u>Second Page</u>
The abstract includes the following paragraphs:

- **Introduction (purpose of your project):** Write an introductory statement giving the reason for your investigation (what you wanted to learn from doing the project).

- **Problem Statement (hypothesis):** Describe what you thought would happen in your experiment.

- **Procedure:** Write a description of how you conducted the experiment. Discuss the variables. It is not important to describe materials used in the experiment unless they were important to your results.

- **Results:** Look at your data. Describe your results. Do not include tables or graphs. Be specific and use numbers. Do not use vague terms such as "most," "nearly all," "a few," or "some."

- **Conclusion:** Summarize the results of the experiment and whether or not the hypothesis was supported by the data collected.

Name: _____ Date: _____

Abstract Organizer

Fill in the blanks below to organize your project information in the correct order. Once you have completed the form, rewrite the abstract. <u>Remember</u>: spelling, grammar, punctuation, neatness, and originality are important.

Paragraph #1: The purpose of my science fair project was (what you wanted to learn)
_____
_____

Paragraph #2: My hypothesis for this project was (give a description of what you thought would happen in your experiment) _____
_____
_____

Paragraph #3: I conducted my experiment by (describe how you carried out the experiment)
_____
_____
_____
_____

The independent variable (factor that changed) in my experiment was _____.
The dependent variable (factor that responded to the change) in my experiment was
_____. I measured the dependent variable in _____
_____

The constants and controls (factors that remained the same) in my experiment were
_____
_____

Paragraph #4: The results of my experiment were (Describe the data you collected. Be specific and use numbers. Do not use vague terms such as "most," "nearly all," "a few," or some.")
_____
_____
_____
_____

Paragraph #5: The results of my experiment show (Summarize the results and whether or not the hypothesis was supported by the data collected.) _____
_____
_____
_____

 **Science Fair Presentation**

You will have a chance to meet and speak with one or more of the science fair judges. Prepare for these interviews to create a positive impression of your project. Plan in advance what you want to say. Write key phrases or ideas on index cards. Take time to rehearse, but don't memorize your presentation. Practice explaining all graphs, tables, your short speech, and answers to possible questions the judges might ask. In this way, you will become familiar and comfortable with your presentation. It is natural to feel a little nervous when giving a presentation. Practice to overcome this feeling.

10 Steps to a Prefect Presentation

Step #1: Smile!

Step #2: Greet the judges and introduce yourself.

Step #3: Give the title of your project and your grade.

Step #4: Tell how you became interested in your topic.

Step #5: Give background information about the topic.

Step #6: Review the main points of your project: purpose, hypothesis, and procedure.

Step #7: Explain the result of your experiment and discuss the variables.

Step #8: Identify the conclusion that you drew from the experiment.

Step #9: Ask the judges if they have any questions.

Step #10: Thank the judges for their time and any suggestions they may have offered to improve your project.

Tips to Help Put You at Ease

- Practice in front of a mirror, your parents, friends, and even the family pet.
- Videotape yourself during practice. You will see the mistakes you made and be able to fix them the next time you speak.
- Practice pointing to diagrams and graphs when you are discussing the results.

Good Manners Count

- Wear nice but comfortable clothes.
- Be polite and practice good manners.
- Make eye contact with your judges.
- Stand up straight and to the side of your exhibit.
- Smile and speak with enthusiasm.
- Speak clearly with an even pace and do not mumble.
- Do not chew gum.
- Keep your hands out of your pockets.
- Do not cross your arms in front of your stomach or chest.

Science Fair Project Ideas

Behavioral Science
Does eye color affect the ability to distinguish between colors in low light?
Does a person's ability to taste differ between fat-free and regular foods?

Botany
Does gravity affect the direction of plant growth?
Does gravity affect seed germination time?

Chemistry
Does temperature affect heat retention in water?
Does the shape of an ice cube affect how quickly it melts?

Computer Science
Does a person's reading retention improve when reading from a computer screen?
Does temperature affect the performance of computer components?

Earth Science
Does Bermuda grass affect the amount of soil runoff?
Does type of water affect how long it holds heat?

Engineering
Does the R Factor of insulation affect how well it insulates?
Does the shape of an object affect the rate at which it sinks?

Environmental Science
Does the presence of detergent in water affect plant growth?
Does the type of material used affect the amount of oil removed from water?

Mathematics
Does a mathematical pattern affect the genre of music being played?
Does the method of stock selection affect portfolio profit?

Medicine and Health
Does caffeine affect blood pressure levels?
Does the fitness level of an athlete affect how fast his/her pulse rate stabilizes?

Microbiology
Does the type of bread affect how fast it molds?
Does caffeine affect the growth rate of bacteria?

Physics
Does water droplet size affect a rainbow's brilliance?
Does temperature affect how high a basketball bounces?

Space Science
Does sunspot activity affect radio reception?
Does the distance from an urban area affect the amount of observed light pollution?

Zoology
Does light affect the chirping rate of a cricket?
Does playing music affect egg-laying in chickens?

Answer Keys

Chapter 1—Scientific Inquiry
Section: Scientific Investigation
The Scientific Method (page 4)
II. 1. What do you want to learn from the experiment?
2. What is already known about the topic?
3. What do you think will happen in the experiment?
4. How will you test the hypothesis and record the results?
5. What do the results tell about the experiment?
6. Do the results support your hypothesis?

Purpose (page 5)
I. 1. Good   2. Too General
3. Too General   4. Good
II. 1. Does temperature affect the growth rate of bread mold?
2. Does a paper towel's texture affect absorbency?
3. Does colored light affect the growth rate of plants?
4. Does light affect the movement of meal worms?
5. Does rust affect the strength of magnets?

Research (page 6)
I. 1. seed, sprout   2. breakfast, memory
II. Answers will vary but might include the following:
Temperature:
1. Why does temperature affect metal?
2. How is the temperature of metal measured?
3. Who uses magnets in extreme temperatures?
4. What effect does temperature have on the properties of metal?
5. When does temperature change the state of metal from a solid to a liquid?
6. Where are magnets used in connection with extreme temperatures?
Magnet:
1. Why are magnets used?
2. How do magnets work?
3. Who in my community would be a good resource?
4. What metals are used to make magnets?
5. When does temperature have an effect on magnets?
6. Where are magnets used?

Hypothesis (page 7)
I. 1. Fertilizer will increase (decrease) the growth rate of a plant.
2. Increased (Decreased) air pressure will increase (decrease) the height a basketball will bounce.
3. Increased age will increase (decrease) the heart rate of humans.
II. 1. Independent: water temperature; Dependent: heart rate of fish
2. Independent: design of the plane; Dependent: distance traveled
3. Independent: amount of light; Dependent: movement of meal worms

Procedure (page 8)
I. 1. c   2. d   3. b   4. a
II. 1. procedure   2. one
3. dependent variable   4. data   5. data table

Data (page 9)
1. 53 cm   2. 67 cm
3. 125 cm   4. 173 cm

Analysis (page 11)
Graph #1: The temperature increased from 12:00 noon to 4:00 P.M. The temperature stayed the same between 4:00 P.M. and 6:00 P.M. and between 8:00 P.M. and 10:00 P.M. The temperature decreased from 6:00 P.M. to 8:00 P.M.
Graph #2: Eight different species ate the corn and millet seeds. Five species ate the thistle seeds. Twelve species ate the sunflower seeds.
Graph #3: The most abundant gas in the atmosphere is nitrogen (78%). The next is oxygen (21%). The category of other gases is the least abundant (1%).

Conclusion (page 12)
I. The results proved that the higher the temperature of the water, the higher the respiration rate of the guppy. The hypothesis was correct.
II. The results proved that the greater the air pressure, the higher a basketball will bounce. The hypothesis was correct.

Section: Scientific Equipment and Measurement
Scientific Measurement (page 14)
I. 1. 48,000 mL   2. 88,000 g   3. 0.108 kg
4. 120 cm   5. 1,400 cm   6. 6,250 mL
7. 0.006 L   8. 950 cm   9. 300 cm
10. 1.5 L
II. 1. L   2. mL
III. 1. mm   2. cm   3. m
IV. 1. kg   2. g

Microscopes (page 16)

I. 1. eyepiece
    2. coarse focus adjustment knob
    3. fine focus adjustment knob
    4. arm   5. base
    6. aperture   7. mirror
    8. body tube   9. nosepiece
    10. objective lenses 11. stage
    12. stage clips   13. diaphragm
II. 1. e   2. d   3. i   4. f   5. a
    6. c   7. b   8. g   9. h

Metric Rulers (page 18)

I.   a. 0.7 cm   b. 1.7 cm   c. 3.2 cm
     d. 5.0 cm   e. 7.0 cm   f. 8.6 cm
III. 1. mm   2. cm   3. m   4. m
     5. km   6. mm   7. m   8. mm
     9. m   10. mm   11. km

Graduated Cylinders (page 20)

I.   a. 1 mL   b. 2 mL   c. 0.5 mL
III. a. 52 mL   b. 65 mL   c. 37 mL   d. 42.5 mL

Balance Scales (page 23)

I.   a. 55 g   b. 11 g
II. 216.5

Thermometers (page 27)

I. 1. 212° Fahrenheit and 100° Celsius
    2. 98.6° Fahrenheit and 37° Celsius
    3. 77° Fahrenheit and 25° Celsius
    4. 32° Fahrenheit and 0° Celsius
II. 1. 32° Fahrenheit
    2. 10° Celsius
    3. -8° Celsius

Note: For all the investigations, answers will vary but should include the following information: the purpose, a brief description of the procedure, and whether or not the hypothesis was supported by the data collected. Expected results are given for each investigation.

Chapter 2—Physical Science

Temperature and Surface Tension (page 30)

The warmer the temperature, the more drops needed to break surface tension.

Calcium and Bones (page 33)

The bones that are exposed to acid become flexible and the texture changes. This is due to the minerals being removed from the bone. The more acidic, the more flexible the bone, and the more bone mass is lost.

Mass and Speed (page 36)

The greater the mass of an object, the greater the speed due to inertia.

Temperature and Elasticity (page 39)

The room-temperature rubber bands were most elastic.

Ultraviolet Light and Sunscreen (page 42)

Answer will depend on brand of sunscreen used. The brand with the highest SPF should produce the least color change in the beads.

Electricity and Lemon Power (page 45)

The 10-gauge wire produces the greatest amount of tingle.

Chapter 3—Life Science

Light and Seed Germination (page 48)

Temperature and moisture are the most important variables in seed germination. Radish seeds do not need light for germination.

Fertilizer and Petunias (page 51)

Fertilizer increases the growth rate of the petunia plants.

DNA Extraction and Onions (page 54)

Murphy's Vegetable Oil Soap™ extracts more DNA.

Chapter 4—Earth and Space Science

pH and Soil (page 57)

Plants grown in soil watered with neutral water will have the best growth rate.

Salinity and Brine Shrimp (page 60)

Water with 10–20 grams of salt added yields the most brine shrimp.

Temperature and Greenhouse Effect (page 63)

The jar of water in the zip-top baggie will have a higher temperature.

Mass and Impact Craters (page 66)

The diameter of the impact crater will increase with the mass of the marble.

BIBLIOGRAPHY

Beaver, John B. and Don Powers. *Electricity and Magnetism: Connecting Students to Science Series.* Quincy, Illinois: Mark Twain Media, Inc., 2003.

Logan, LaVerne and Don Powers. *Atmosphere and Weather: Connecting Students to Science Series.* Quincy, Illinois: Mark Twain Media, Inc., 2002.

Logan, LaVerne. *Rocks and Minerals: Connecting Students to Science Series.* Quincy, Illinois: Mark Twain Media, Inc., 2002.

Logan, LaVerne. *Sound: Connecting Students to Science Series.* Quincy, Illinois: Mark Twain Media, Inc., 2003.

Olson, Steve and Susan Loucks-Horsley. *Inquiry and the National Science Education Standards: A Guide for Teaching and Learning.* Washington, D.C.: National Academies Press, 2000.

Powers, Don and John B. Beaver. *The Solar System: Connecting Students to Science Series.* Quincy, Illinois: Mark Twain Media, Inc., 2004.

Raham, Gary. *Science Tutor: Earth and Space Science.* Quincy, Illinois: Mark Twain Media, Inc., 2006.

Raham, Gary. *Science Tutor: Life Science.* Quincy, Illinois: Mark Twain Media, Inc., 2006.

Sandall, Barbara R. *Chemistry: Connecting Students to Science Series.* Quincy, Illinois: Mark Twain Media, Inc., 2002.

Sandall, Barbara R. *Light and Color: Connecting Students to Science Series.* Quincy, Illinois: Mark Twain Media, Inc., 2003.

Sciencesaurus: A Student Handbook. Houghton Mifflin, 2002.

"Science Fair Project Ideas." Science Buddies. 23 January 2009. < http://www.sciencebuddies.org/science-fair-projects/project_guide_index.shtml>

Shireman, Myrl. *Physical Science.* Quincy, Illinois: Mark Twain Media, Inc., 1997.